"Why Do I Get the Feeling You're Trying to Distrust Me?"

Simon asked.

"That's not true. I'm simply doing my job."

Very deliberately he glanced at his watch. "It's after five. You're off duty."

"You know perfectly well that isn't how things work at my level of responsibility. Or do you believe I should simply turn off my brain when I'm with you and simper prettily?" She was stung by his sarcasm and felt driven to respond in kind.

"It might be a refreshing alternative to the third degree," Simon snapped. "You're a woman, Allegra, and I'm a man, and we happen to be very attracted to each other. That's what it comes down to."

Dear Reader:

There is an electricity between two people in love that makes everything they do magic, larger than life. This is what we bring you in SILHOUETTE INTIMATE MOMENTS.

SILHOUETTE INTIMATE MOMENTS are longer, more sensuous romance novels filled with adventure, suspense, glamor or melodrama. These books have an element no one else has tapped: excitement.

We are proud to present the very best romance has to offer from the very best romance writers. In the coming months look for some of your favorite authors such as Elizabeth Lowell, Nora Roberts, Erin St. Claire and Brooke Hastings.

SILHOUETTE INTIMATE MOMENTS are for the woman who wants more than she has ever had before. These books are for you.

Meredith Morgan,
Silhouette Books,
320 Steelcase Rd., East,
Markham, Ontario
L3R 2M1

Silver Zephyr
Maura Seger

Silhouette Intimate Moments
Published by Silhouette Books New York

Distributed in Canada by PaperJacks Ltd., a Licensee
of the trademarks of Simon & Schuster, Inc.

Silhouette Books by Maura Seger

A Gift Beyond Price (SE #135)
Silver Zephyr (IM #61)

SILHOUETTE BOOKS, a Division of Simon & Schuster, Inc.
1230 Avenue of the Americas, New York, N.Y. 10020
In Canada distributed by PaperJacks Ltd.,
330 Steelcase Road, Markham, Ontario

Distributed by Pocket Books

ISBN: 0-671-49644-1

First Silhouette Books printing August, 1984

10 9 8 7 6 5 4 3 2 1

Printed in Canada

Silver
Zephyr

Chapter 1

"I'LL HAVE TO SEE SOME IDENTIFICATION, MISS. ONLY passengers and guests are allowed on the field."

Allegra Whitney reached into her calfskin purse on the car seat beside her and withdrew the silver folder holding her ticket. She knew the precautions were necessary, but they were still an annoyance. The thin gold watch on her wrist told her that she was running some fifteen minutes late. That wasn't like her.

"Here you are."

The guard checked her ticket carefully, then handed it back with a smile. "Thank you, miss. Have a good trip."

Allegra nodded pleasantly. The young man's professional demeanor couldn't be faulted, but he hadn't been entirely able to hide a note of skepticism. Not that she blamed him. Plenty of people thought those making this trip were crazy; that was part of its attraction.

A corner of the former Long Island potato field was set aside for passenger parking. She left the burgandy Mercedes there, amid a collection of Porsches, Jaguars and BMWs, accepted a receipt from the respectful attendant, and arranged for a porter to take her luggage on board.

As she walked away from the car the slim heels of her handmade pumps sank slightly into the soft ground. She didn't mind. She had discovered that one of the great advantages of buying only the best was that it was always tougher than it looked.

Like her. At twenty-eight she had the tall, elegant carriage of a thoroughbred. Despite the rigorous demands of running her own public relations firm, she always found the time to stay in good shape.

Her body was slender, but curved in all the right places. Smooth, apricot-tinged skin and glossy chestnut hair proclaimed her vitality. Her hazel eyes, set beneath arching brows, were wide and clear. Superb bone structure would give her beauty even when she grew old. Her cheekbones were high, her nose straight and slim, and her chin gently rounded.

She carried herself with an innate pride that was, with the good humor reflected by her uptilted mouth, her most noteworthy characteristic. Confidence in her own abilities, added to a willingness to take neither herself nor the rest of the world too seriously, was responsible in large measure for her success.

She had come a great distance from the skinny little

girl growing up in a Brooklyn tenement and the self-conscious young woman plodding her way through City University. The elite world of the wealthy and powerful was her home now, but she had never lost sight of her roots.

For the first time since getting up that morning in her Manhattan duplex, Allegra paused to take a deep breath and relax for a moment. It was liable to be the last quiet she knew for two weeks, and she wanted to make the most of it.

At the far edge of the field, above a brace of ancient oak trees, the sun was setting in a blaze of purple and orange. The day had been hot and humid, typical for New York in the summer. But the temperature was at last beginning to fall.

A fresh breeze blew from the east, carrying the scents of salt water, marshes and pine forests. It ruffled the skirt of her ivory linen suit and stirred the collar of the persimmon silk shirt she wore beneath it.

Allegra frowned for a moment as she realized the direction of the onshore wind. Would that be a problem? A page from the manual she had studied so intensively swam before her: The acceleration control systems maintain an average speed of thirty-five knots against headwinds not in excess of eighty miles per hour. Twin turbojets and internal pressurization controls assure stability superior to that of conventional air or sea craft.

Translation: Nothing short of a hurricane can rattle a wine glass.

Which was just as well, considering that the passengers gathering in the Long Island potato field were used to the ultimate in comfort and service and would not take kindly to anything that rumpled their Dior silk shirts or smudged their Gucci loafers.

Yet they still wanted adventure, wanted to feel that they were part of something new and exciting. Because she could offer them that combination of luxury and daring, Allegra's public relations job had been made relatively easy. She could only hope it would remain that way once the voyage actually began.

She was pleased to note that the media were out in force. A battery of television cameras was lined up along one side of the field, and several well-recognized correspondents were on hand. So were the notorious *paparazzi*, but they were contained behind a fence.

Ordinarily she would have stopped to speak with the reporters. Besides the fact that she knew and liked most of them, it was part of her job. But just then she was in a hurry and had to be satisfied to note that several members of her firm were moving among the group, making sure that everything went smoothly.

As she began walking toward the boarding ramp another car entered the parking area. Her glance fell on it appreciatively. Vintage 1930s Bugattis in mint condition were rare even in her exalted circles. She found herself wondering what sort of person had the imagination to own such an extraordinary car.

Her curiosity was quickly satisfied. From behind the wheel stepped a tall, lean man dressed in well-worn jeans, a white button-down shirt that looked like a retread from his business wardrobe and cowboy boots.

To a casual observer he appeared startlingly out of place amid the expensively garbed crowd. But Allegra, who understood the peculiarities of the wealthy, wasn't fooled for a moment.

The jeans were defiantly nondesigner, the kind that could be picked up in any dry goods store out West. But the belt that held them around a taut waist was of the finest leather and set with a beautifully crafted silver and turquoise clasp. The shirt was standard issue from one of the most exclusive and expensive men's shops in the world. Its sleeves were rolled up to reveal corded forearms that went well with what looked to be a very good body indeed.

His deeply tanned skin was an interesting contrast to thick, slightly curly brown hair that glistened with the gold of the sun. His face was broad and powerfully made, his features rough-hewn, as though not completely finished. Not that there was anything lacking in him. On the contrary, he had the self-contained expression of a great hunting bird—a hawk, perhaps, or a condor—surveying its domain before selecting its prey.

From behind wire-rim glasses, the man's eyes abruptly met hers. She saw a flicker of surprise before it was quickly masked behind a gleam of purely male interest. He looked her up and down slowly, just as she had done him, and was apparently satisfied by what he saw.

Allegra forced herself not to look away. Her life was built on the acceptance of challenges. She had no doubt that was exactly what the man represented, and she

wasn't about to let him intimidate her. Not even when
he turned his luggage over to the porter and abruptly
strode toward her.

"You are," his deep, faintly amused voice inquired,
"a passenger, I hope?"

She forced herself to nod coolly. "In a manner of
speaking. My public relations firm represents the *Silver
Zephyr,* so it seemed sensible for me to go along on the
maiden voyage."

" 'Sensible' is not precisely how I would describe
anyone's participation in this little jaunt," he drawled,
"but I suppose it will do." Without warning he held
out a hand and smiled. The effect was devastating. In
an instant he was transformed from a rather conde-
scending member of the upper crust to an extraordinari-
ly attractive and approachable man.

"Simon York," he said as she automatically gave
him her hand. His touch was firm but gentle, his skin
dry and warm. Glancing down, she saw that his fingers
were long and square-tipped, lightly dusted with the
same golden hair she saw on his arms. She wondered if
he was like that all over. . . .

A warning bell went off in her head. Her eyes met
his with careful directness. Her smile was cool and
deliberately professional. "Allegra Whitney. It's a
pleasure to meet you, Mr. York. I hope you'll enjoy the
voyage."

He raised a thick, slashing eyebrow sardonically, the
gesture telling her that she wasn't going to get rid of
him that easily. "You meant it when you said 'my'
firm. Whitney Public Relations is well known. I knew

a woman ran it, but I had no idea you were so young. You must be damn good at your job.''

Despite herself, Allegra was knocked a bit off balance mentally. She was used to her success attracting curiosity and even envy. Those she coped with matter-of-factly. But Simon York's manner implied something more.

On one level he seemed to genuinely mean what he said. She sensed he was a man secure enough in himself to never be put off by any woman's credentials, however impressive.

But on another, deeper level she got the feeling that the two of them were sharing a joke, as though it was already understood that none of the superficial aspects of their identities meant anything in what was going to be a very personal relationship.

Accustomed though she was to rolling with the punches, that was a bit too much, too soon. ''Thank you,'' she said coolly, disengaging her hand. The sudden lack of his touch made her feel curiously bereft and further stiffened her resistance. ''I really must be going.''

Far from being put off, he only seemed to become more amused. ''Fine with me, since we're going to the same place.'' Falling into step beside her, he ignored her nettled glance and gestured toward what was to be their home for the next two weeks.

''Really something, isn't it?''

With all that could be said about the *Silver Zephyr*— news stories about it had waxed eloquent with such phrases as ''the revival of a dream,'' ''the epitome of

romance and daring,'' and so on—to refer to it simply
as ''something'' seemed like a deliberate put-down.

Allegra wondered if he might be one of those men
who always needed to feel superior to their surroundings, but she dismissed that thought the instant it
passed through her mind.

Simon York was far too innately confident to indulge
in any such ploy. It was much likelier that he merely
had mixed feelings about the voyage they were about to
embark on. Which led, naturally enough, to the question of why he was going.

''Is this a vacation for you?''

He cast her a surprised glance. ''Why do you ask?''

She frowned. People who answered a question with
a question were not high on her list of favorites. ''Oh,
just because you don't seem to be looking forward to
the trip very much.''

Simon stopped at the foot of the gangplank and
glanced up . . . and up . . . and up . . . along the full
height of the shimmering immensity floating before
them. ''How,'' he retorted, ''could anyone not be
looking forward to that?''

Allegra followed his gaze, the rhythm of her heart
instantly increasing. She had been on board the *Silver
Zephyr* half a dozen times during its final outfittings
and had been one of a dozen passengers privileged to
sail on the shakedown voyage. But none of that had
lessened her awe of the majestic craft that challenged
both the skies and the limits of human imagination.

On the contrary, she marveled all the more at the
engineers and dreamers who had dared to build what

was at once a reminder of a vanished age and a glimpse of what the future might hold.

Quietly she said, "It's magnificent."

"It's big all right. I'll give you that."

Allegra couldn't help but laugh. "Are you always given to such understatement? That's fifteen acres of high-density polyurethane covering the aluminum keel. Tens of thousands of pounds of helium were needed to fill it. We have room for some five hundred and twenty passengers, not to mention twice that number in crew, as well as ample space for cargo and supplies."

"Very impressive," Simon murmured dryly.

"It's meant to be. The *Silver Zephyr* is a marriage of the sumptuous ocean liners of a bygone era and the jets that have eclipsed them."

"You sound as though you're quoting from the advertising brochure."

Not at all abashed, she nodded. "I may be, since I wrote it."

He grinned down at her, causing another rapid acceleration of her heartbeat, and rattled off from memory, "You will sail through a sea of air only a few thousand feet above the water, enjoying both your sumptuous surroundings and the beauties of nature seen from a perspective few have ever known."

"I'm flattered. It never occurred to me that anyone would remember my words so accurately."

"Let's just say I studied the brochure carefully before deciding to sign on."

"Then the bargain rates had nothing to do with it?"

He snorted. "Hardly. This oversized balloon costs

only slightly less than the Concorde, which I happen to think is grossly overpriced.''

So did Allegra, but she wasn't about to admit as much. Stiffly she said, "Calling the *Silver Zephyr* a balloon is like calling a diamond a piece of coal. The accommodations and service on board are unmatched even in the world's top hotels.''

"They should be,'' he shot back. "About the only sensible elements this venture has going for it are the incredibly low energy costs and the ability to transport cargo far more quickly and cheaply than any ship. On a dollars-and-cents basis, your success should be assured.''

"But you're not sure it is?''

He shrugged, watching a whippet-thin model and teeth-flashing designer start up the gangway. They were laughing uproariously as they posed for the eager photographers who clustered at the bottom.

"There is another aspect to consider,'' Simon said quietly, "which may account for the . . . shall we say reckless attitude of our fellow passengers. Don't you sense a certain 'live for today and let the devil take tomorrow' mood?''

Allegra stifled a sigh. She had known the subject would come up sooner or later, but hadn't quite expected to be confronted by it before she even got on board. Softly, so that there was no chance of being overheard, she said, "I presume you're referring to the completely unfounded fears some people have about the safety of dirigibles?''

"You can't deny it's a problem.''

"No, but only because the crash of the *Hindenburg* fifty years ago put a stop to the development of the technology. Until now. The *Silver Zephyr* is without a doubt one of the safest transportation systems ever devised. We use helium for inflation, instead of the *Hindenburg*'s hydrogen, so we're completely nonflammable. And every one of our navigational and control systems has triple backups. Compared to us, planes are a crap shoot and your own car is a death trap."

Simon looked faintly amused, but he wasn't disagreeing. "You don't have to sell me on that. The basic technology is sound. If I thought otherwise, I wouldn't be here."

Then why, Allegra wondered again, did she get the impression that he would rather have been elsewhere? Granted, the men and women streaming on board might have some niggling doubts about the wisdom of what they were doing, but at least they seemed intent on enjoying it. Simon, on the other hand, seemed downright serious. Or perhaps that was just his manner.

As he stood aside so she could precede him up the gangway, Allegra glanced back at him. He had paused for a moment and was surveying the craft again, this time with the piercing intensity she had sensed the first moment she saw him.

Even as she told herself not to let her imagination run away with her, she was certain that something about the magnificent airship troubled Simon. She itched to ask him flat out what the problem might be, but discretion got the better of her.

This was not the time or place for such a discussion, and he was not a man who seemed to welcome too much curiosity about his inner thoughts. Besides, there were other far more immediate matters that required her attention.

At the top of the gangway passengers stepped onto moving sidewalks which sloped gently upward toward the main deck, where uniformed stewards checked off names and gave directions to cabins.

Once inside, the similarity between the dirigible and a cruise ship was very noticeable. Three decks spanned the upper reaches above the cargo bays and crew quarters. Two were given over to luxurious cabins, while the topmost housed the recreational and dining facilities.

Huge plate-glass windows provided magnificent views of the countryside. For those who wanted a closer look, there was an enclosed deck or, better still, the observation platform suspended from the under-carriage.

Like a great ship, the *Silver Zephyr* was a self-contained world complete with library, movie theater, health spa, swimming pool, night club and so on. But unlike any vessel confined to the seas, it could move at will over land, providing an immediate bridge for its passengers to the great cities of Europe and beyond.

After the steward had told them both how to find their cabins, Allegra turned to Simon and gave him one of her polite dismissal smiles. "I'm sure you won't have any trouble finding your way around, Mr. York, so if you'll excuse me, I'm needed elsewhere."

His firm, rather appealing mouth twitched slightly. "I'm sure you are, Ms. Whitney. Don't let me detain you. However, perhaps we could get together for a drink before dinner?"

Allegra hesitated a moment. She wasn't sure she wanted any more contact with the disturbing Mr. York than she was unable to avoid. He did things to her concentration and equilibrium that she was not used to. On the other hand, it was her job to help make the voyage a success. Being churlish to one of the passengers was hardly a good way to start.

"All right. Shall we say the Sky Lounge at eight o'clock?"

He nodded, then flashed her another of those devastating smiles before taking himself off down the long corridor leading to the plushest suites.

Allegra made her way to the captain's office, frowning slightly. Something about Simon York didn't ring true. He had booked one of the most expensive cabins available on a voyage he didn't seem to really want to take. He was obviously wealthy and accustomed to authority, yet she had never heard of him.

That in itself was surprising. Without giving herself any undue credit, she knew she was exceptionally well informed about who could and could not afford to indulge in such a venture as the *Silver Zephyr*'s maiden journey.

She had made it her business, very successfully, to know the small group of men and women who were the movers and shakers of society. The trend-setters, innovators, celebrities, self-made millionaires and wealthy scions who established the standards by which so many others tried to live. It was a relatively small list, and Simon York was most definitely not on it.

So who was he? On her way down the plushly carpeted hallway, she considered and rejected in short order such possibilities as con man, gigolo, jewel thief and card shark. If he were any or all of those things, he would have taken pains to blend in more effectively with the opulent crowd instead of standing out so assertively.

She knew she had never met him before; he would have remained quite firmly in her memory. Yet she couldn't dismiss the faint hint of recollection his name caused.

Perhaps Winston Goodfellow would have some idea. After knocking on the door of the captain's office, she opened it and strolled in. A large mahogany desk dominated a room that might have been lifted intact from a sailing vessel of the previous century. Glancing around, Allegra reflected that there was a good deal of Winston's personality in evidence. He had clearly made himself comfortable, which was the best possible sign that he intended to remain.

The straight-backed, iron-haired man speaking with a young officer looked perfectly at home in the pristine white uniform he wore like a second skin. Hardly surprising, since Captain Goodfellow had spent his entire adult life in regulation dress of one sort or another.

He had grown up in England, where his diplomat parents were stationed, then returned to the States to serve as a naval officer and pilot in Korea and Vietnam.

His most recent years had been spent flying for one of the major international airlines, until he was lured away to become master of the *Silver Zephyr*.

That he was master could not be doubted. He had participated directly in every stage of design and construction, and knew the great craft better than almost anyone else. Allegra could not imagine a better choice for captain, and she had not hesitated to tell him so.

Glancing up, Winston caught sight of her and raised a hand, dismissing the young officer. "Ah, my dear, come in. I was just preparing to go up to the bridge."

"Then everything is on schedule?"

"Did you doubt it? The mooring ropes will be loosed at precisely eight P.M., as planned."

"And woe betide any late arrivals."

"Precisely. Coffee?"

"Thanks. The boarding seems to be going smoothly."

"Well enough. We've had the overflow from several rather raucous bon voyage parties, and a couple of photographers tried to sneak past security. But other than that, there haven't been any problems."

"Good. I know they're bound to crop up on any maiden voyage, but the more we can avoid, the better."

"I run a tight ship, Allegra. You know that."

"You'll have to, with this bunch. Have you seen them?"

He winced slightly, his patrician brow furrowing. "Enough. Any chance they'll settle down a bit once we're underway?"

"Yes, I think so. Provided we can convince them that they're not going to be blown out of the sky at any moment."

Shaking his head impatiently, Winston muttered, "The abysmal stupidity of the human race never fails to astound me. They couldn't be safer if they were in their mothers' arms."

"Just keep in mind that they expect a bit more excitement than they'd find there."

"Once we get to the Continent, they'll have plenty to do."

"That's true. But on the way we have to keep them all well fed and entertained." She paused a moment before asking gently, "Have you reconciled yourself yet to the need for a captain's table?"

He sighed morosely. "I suppose, though I have to admit that's one thing about this job that doesn't delight me. With World Air all I had to do was make an occasional announcement about the splendid mountains on the left or some other such nonsense."

"I'm afraid it's a bit more involved this time. But you won't have any problem." Smiling, she stirred her coffee as she told him honestly, "I can't imagine anyone more urbane. You'll do the job perfectly."

"Of course," he sniffed before answering her smile with his own. "At least, I'll try, but I can't possibly be more charming than you, Allegra. You'd put a duchess to shame."

Touched by his unexpected praise, she flushed slightly. Winston might look and act like an aristocrat, but in fact his experiences in two wars had made him a hardheaded survivor with the rare capacity to genuinely care about others. At fifty-eight he was a widower with two grown children who adored him and a host of true friends scattered around the world.

Since their first meeting six months before, he and Allegra had progressed from the cordial regard of two professionals who recognized each other's abilities to genuine affection. She trusted him, enough to ask him about what was still uppermost in her mind.

"Winston . . . have you ever heard of a man named Simon York?"

He frowned and thought for a moment. "It rings a bell, but I can't place it. Why do you ask?"

"He's a passenger. I met him as I was arriving. He strikes me as . . . different somehow."

A silvery eyebrow was raised quizzically. "Oh? Far be it from me to suggest everyone should march to the same drummer, but is this difference of his likely to cause trouble?"

"I don't see how. In fact, it's probably just in my mind. There's something about him . . ." She broke off, abruptly aware that Winston's expression had changed. Instead of looking concerned, he was eyeing her benignly.

"Do go on. This is just getting interesting."

"There's nothing more to say. I just wondered if you knew anything about him."

"No, but if you're really curious, I can radio the home office and make inquiries."

Allegra was tempted, but nonetheless she shook her head. "We don't have any right to intrude on Mr. York's privacy. He hasn't done anything to warrant that."

"My dear, your scruples are admirable, but so are your instincts. If you have any feeling that this man might be up to no good on *my* ship, I would very much appreciate your telling me."

"Now don't get huffy, Winston. My guess is we have less to worry about from Simon than from any number of other passengers. This is, after all, not exactly a sedate bunch."

"If it were up to me, we'd have bed checks and a curfew." He shivered slightly. "God only knows what sort of things they've brought on board. If we don't have at least one drunken brawl and a drug overdose before the voyage is over, I'll be astonished."

"Don't be so pessimistic. Anyone would think you were looking for trouble."

"What else can be expected from a crowd of over-aged, overindulged delinquents?" he parried.

"They aren't all like that. We're privileged to have on board some of the most respected and powerful people in the country. Men and women we want to impress so they will trust us with their business, particularly cargo. You know as well as I do that's where the real profit is."

"I suppose," he grumbled. "But the rest of them had better toe the line. I intend to have an uneventful voyage."

Allegra couldn't help but giggle, a rare occurrence for her. "You make that sound like a threat, but I have to admit I'm in agreement. If we can bring the *Silver Zephyr* back here fourteen days from now with everyone and everything in as good condition as right now, I'll be delighted."

"A worthwhile goal, my dear." Setting down his bone china cup, he rose and bowed ceremoniously. "But before we can conclude a successful voyage, we have to begin it. So I'd best get up to the bridge. Care to come along?"

The invitation surprised her. Winston did not go in for a lot of extra bodies cluttering up his command center. Reluctantly, she shook her head. "No, thanks. I'd better get settled in."

"As you wish. I trust I'll see you at dinner?"

"Would I leave you to the wolves, Winston?"

"My dear," he murmured, holding the door open for her, "any wolves on board are far more likely to be after you than me."

"Not the ones in designer evening gowns. They'll be after you like a shot."

Pleased, though he tried to hide it, he inclined his head gravely. "Then we'll just have to protect each other. You keep an eye out for overeager females, and I'll ward off Mr. Simon York."

Allegra smiled her agreement before they parted in the corridor, but as she made her way to her cabin she found herself wondering who she really wanted to be protected from: the inscrutable Simon or herself.

Chapter 2

HER LUGGAGE WAS WAITING FOR HER WHEN ALLEGRA reached her cabin. She took a quick glance around, noting the finishing touches added since she had last occupied the room during the shakedown cruise.

The walls were now papered in a silvery brocade that went well with the Aubusson carpet in muted shades of blue and rose. The king-size bed with its ornately carved headboard was covered by a spread that picked up the same colors and matched the curtains hanging at the large picture windows.

An antique armoire stood against one wall, while a mirrored dresser took up part of another. The furniture was large and solid without being in the least ungainly. It suited the spacious dimensions of the room.

Baroque moldings decorated the high ceiling from which a crystal chandelier hung. Filigreed wall sconces bracketed the archway leading to the dressing room fitted out with cedar-lined closets and drawers. On the other side was the bath, a sybarite's delight, with marble shower, steam cabinet, heat lamps and a sunken tub framed—for some unknown reason—by flowing gauze drapes.

With a wry smile Allegra considered that this so-called cabin was in fact far bigger than the first apartment she had been able to manage on her own. And it was by no means the most luxurious accommodation available on board the *Silver Zephyr*. The royal suite alone comprised four rooms plus a private enclosed deck and sauna.

The planners and decorators could never be accused of simple tastes, but neither had they really gone overboard. Opulence was expected by their demanding clientele.

So was the ultimate in pampering. A discreet peal of the doorbell, which chimed to the tune of Gershwin's "Rhapsody in Blue," announced the arrival of the maid offering to unpack for her. Allegra politely refused, preferring to take care of that task for herself and knowing that the woman would be busy enough elsewhere.

She spent the next few minutes putting away her clothes, confirming that none of the practical but suitably glamorous items she had selected needed to be pressed, and deciding what to wear that evening.

After slipping out of her suit and blouse, she put them away and padded into the bathroom to start filling the tub. A handful of fragrant crystals turned the water blue and perfumed the room with the scent of jasmine.

Allegra removed the rest of her clothes, then slipped gratefully into the silky warmth and laid her head back against the pillowed edge.

Breathing in slowly, she began the ritual of relaxation that always served her so well. One by one she stilled the levels of thought until all the little voices in her mind were at last silent.

With that tranquility came a draining of tension out of her body. Muscles she had not even realized were taut relaxed. Her breathing grew deeper and slower. She let her arms go limp and float to the surface of the water.

For long, renewing moments she hovered on the edge of sleep, confident that she would not slip over, and savoring the absolute sense of peace she had attained. There were times in her hectic world when the ability to slip away like this was all that kept her sane. She let nothing interfere with it.

Until now. Without warning a thought sparked far in the depths of her consciousness: Simon York. Allegra frowned. She didn't want to think about him, or anything. But it seemed she had no choice.

Shifting restlessly, she replayed her encounter with the man who seemed so firmly lodged in her mind. What was it about him that she found so fascinating? Granted he was compellingly attractive in an unusual way. Not the pretty-boy handsomeness of male models or screen heartthrobs, but the tough, unadorned strength of a man well equipped to deal with an often hostile world.

She knew without having to be told that Simon was not a man to cross. Yet there was far more to him than rugged determination. He challenged her intelligence as well as her femininity.

His swift perception and the flashes of humor she had seen in his light gray eyes told her that he was a man to appreciate on far more than simply a physical level. She was willing to bet he would make a good friend, and a bad enemy.

Now why should she be thinking about what kind of enemy Simon would make? Her imagination really was running away with her. They were about to embark on the ultimate pleasure cruise, with all worldly cares left behind. Speaking of which, if she didn't want to miss the launch, she would have to hustle.

Stepping out of the tub, she reached for a bath sheet and wrapped it around herself before padding over to the mirror. With swift, sure strokes she smoothed her hair into a neat chignon at the nape of her neck, then lightly applied a foundation and blusher before doing her eyes.

They were her best feature, and she had no hesitation about playing them up. By the time she had outlined her mouth with a lip pencil and brushed on a rose gloss, only a few minutes were left.

Wearing fresh lingerie and high-heeled evening sandals, she slipped the mauve knit over her head and wiggled it into place before glancing at herself in the dressing room's full-length mirror.

The dress was deceptively simple. Woven of a mulberry cotton and silk blend, it weighed only a few ounces and looked, on its hanger, like little more than a tube of material.

But with her inside it the impression changed drasti-

cally. The dress clung to the high, firm curves of her
breasts, the slender indentation of her waist and her
gently rounded hips before slipping sleekly down
tapered legs to her ankles.

High-necked and long-sleeved, from the front it
seemed to cover her completely, until she moved. Then
the slit up one side revealed the honey-toned expanse of
her leg clear to her thigh. The low-cut back bared her
almost to the curve of her bottom.

It was a deliberately dramatic dress, one that made
people look twice and again. Allegra wore it with
confidence, sure of her innate elegance and her ability
to deal with the attention it provoked.

Or at least she had always felt that way in the past.
As she dabbed on a few drops of her favorite perfume,
she found herself wondering what Simon would make
of her appearance.

Dropping the key into her evening purse, she turned
away from her door and joined the people heading
toward the observation lounge, where a festive air
prevailed.

As a popular rock band played and champagne corks
popped, the glittering crowd seemed intent on outdoing
each other. Rarely could Allegra remember seeing a
more lavish display of designer creations and jewels,
on both the men and women.

She paused at the entrance and smiled wryly, feeling
for just a moment like the outsider she had once been.
Then she mentally straightened her shoulders and
waded in.

Circulating among the guests, most of whom she
knew, she was not at first aware of the man watching

her. Not until an almost imperceptible shiver ran down her spine did she turn to find Simon slouched against a nearby wall, eyeing her appreciatively.

He had changed into evening clothes, not the glitzy velvets and laces favored by some of the men, but the traditional white and black attire that only served to emphasize the devastating effect of his masculinity. Against the brilliant white of his shirt, his burnished skin looked even darker than before, and the golden glints of his hair shone clearly.

Allegra couldn't help but notice that she was not the only one impressed by his appearance. From the corner of her eye, she glimpsed several women and—the times being what they were—a couple of men whose interest was obviously stirred.

But Simon paid her the compliment of being apparently oblivious to them. Straightening his big body, he strode toward her with easy grace and smiled lazily. "Glad you could make it."

"Oh, I wouldn't have missed the launch for anything."

He grinned down at her, not at all put off by the implication that she had no particular eagerness to see him again. Taking her arm in a gesture she told herself only seemed possessive, he steered her toward the bar. "Let's get a drink. Then you can explain to me why the launch is being held at night."

"That's simple. It's far more dramatic this way. We'll rise into the sky silhouetted against the moon which, in case you haven't noticed, is full. That was also a deliberate choice." She laughed softly as he placed a glass of champagne in her hand. "If it had turned out to be cloudy we would have been terribly disappointed.''

''I can imagine. It sounds as though even more planning went into this than I had realized.''

''Down to the last little detail. I'm not embarrassed to admit that we're milking this launch for everything it's worth. Good publicity is literally priceless.''

''Sort of free advertising?''

''Exactly.''

He looked at her over the rim of his glass. ''But only if everything goes right.''

''Everything will,'' she assured him firmly. ''Nothing's been left to chance. My firm even arranged for the lights of the Empire State Building to blink on and off as we pass over it.''

Simon looked puzzled. ''Not to nitpick, but isn't that in the opposite direction from where we're going?''

''We're making a ceremonial fly-by of New York before heading out to sea,'' Allegra explained. ''Sort of a salute to the city that is the *Silver Zephyr*'s home port.''

''Makes sense. You'll be seen by millions.''

''That's the idea. Plus the passengers will have an incredible view of the city. We'll be flying at the altitude of a helicopter, but far more slowly, so they'll have time to savor the experience.''

''I'm all in favor of that,'' Simon informed her blandly, his eyes never leaving hers. ''There are definitely some experiences in life meant to be relished slowly and thoroughly.''

The words themselves were innocuous enough, but his look was not. Allegra could feel the heat rising to her cheeks and cursed inwardly. Her expressive features were occasionally the bane of her existence. She had the feeling that Simon knew exactly what was going through her mind and was enjoying every moment of it.

Exasperated more with herself than with him, she said, "They're about to release the mooring ropes. Let's get a spot by the windows."

He nodded and once again took her arm. Allegra was surprised by how readily she was becoming accustomed to his touch. The brush of his fingers was warm and gentle through the thin fabric of her dress. She could feel the slight roughness of the callused tips and wondered what sort of work he did to leave such evidence.

"Are you from this area?" she asked as they found a couple of seats with a good view.

He shook his head. "Farther west. I've been living in California the last few years."

"What do you do out there?"

"This and that. I'm an engineer."

Now why did she get the feeling that he was deliberately trying to make his work seem boring? It wasn't just the laconic answers but the flatness with which they were offered. Simon York was not inviting inquiries into his existence.

With no compulsion about thwarting him, she said, "That must be fascinating. Tell me about it."

He shrugged dismissively. "There's nothing to tell. I followed the same route as a lot of other people with similar backgrounds and ended up working in computers." His eyes narrowed slightly, roaming over her with casual male ease. "I'm sure we can find something more interesting to talk about. You, for instance. How did you get involved in public relations?"

Peeved by his refusal to reveal even a small part of himself to her, she said, "I followed the same route as a lot of other people with similar backgrounds."

Simon stared at her for a moment before he suddenly laughed and shook his head admiringly. "Okay, I deserved that. It's just that I really do think a lot of people find my work boring, and I hate to inflict it on them. Yours, on the other hand, seems genuinely interesting."

"It can be," she agreed. "I've met some fascinating people over the years." She wasn't about to tell him that even on such short acquaintance he looked to be among that select group. "And I've been involved in events I could never have been part of otherwise."

"Like this?"

"Exactly, although I have to admit that when I first heard about the *Silver Zephyr*, I thought the idea was crazy."

"What happened to change your mind?"

"Learning more about it. The guiding light behind the project, Tristan Ward, gave me an intensive course in the joys of dirigibles. He was so convincing and so eloquent that I finally caved in and agreed to be part of the team." She frowned slightly. "Tristan's the heart and soul of this project. It's a shame he couldn't make the voyage."

"Oh, why not?"

"He was hurt in an auto accident a couple of days ago."

"There's a certain irony in that. A man who could create something as daring as an airship getting hurt in something as mundane as a car."

"I'm sure Tristan thinks so. Anyway, he knows he can trust all the rest of us to do everything possible to make the trip a success."

"He's a lucky man to have associates he can trust."

Allegra raised a slender eyebrow. "Do I detect a rueful note there?"

He laughed, lifting his glass to her. "You're very perceptive. Yes, I have had a couple of run-ins with colleagues, or, more correctly, with the people you sometimes have to deal with to get an idea off the ground."

"You mean the money men?"

"That's right. I know venture capitalists are essential to the start-up of any new business, but sometimes they can be a real pain in the . . ."

She nodded thoughtfully. Tristan had expressed some doubts about that aspect of the venture. His capital had come essentially from three men, all of whom he seemed to get along with well enough. But there had still been problems, little things that didn't matter by themselves but added up to a lot of aggravation.

"I guess I'm lucky to be in a line of work that required relatively little investment to start up," she said thoughtfully.

"What prompted you to start your own business?"

That was a question she was often asked, and one she had long since developed a pat answer for. But it seemed to have temporarily slipped her mind. Slowly she said, "I was impatient to prove myself. Working for someone else would have taken too long."

"But you must have gotten experience somewhere?"

"Oh, sure. I started out working part-time in college as a typist at a public relations firm. When I graduated I was hired as a junior associate." She smiled reminiscently. "Very junior. In the year and a half that I was with the firm, I practically lived on the premises. People accused me of saving on rent by stowing a cot in the closet."

He grinned understandingly. "Ambitious, were you?"

"That's putting it mildly." A shadow flitted across her face. She wasn't about to tell him what her single-minded drive had done to her social life.

Early on she had discovered that the men she met wanted the best of both worlds: a woman who was emotionally and financially self-sufficient, yet ready to cater to their every whim and wait on them hand and foot. She wasn't about to fall into that trap, not while she had her own goals to fulfill.

Simon leaned forward. Without warning his big hand covered hers as their eyes met. "Most people have no idea what it's like to want something so badly that no amount of hard work or heartache can turn you off it. At the risk of sounding ruthless, I have to say that's their loss. A woman like yourself, who's willing to put everything on the line, is very special."

Though she automatically searched his words for some sign of sarcasm or phoniness, she could detect none. He seemed to genuinely mean what he said. Was that possible? Had she finally met a man who could applaud her determination rather than demean it?

Her smile was a bit shaky as she said, "Sounds to me like you've had a pretty tough road yourself. Are you still claiming to be just a run-of-the-mill engineer?"

He sat back and took a swallow of his champagne before shaking his head ruefully. "I guess there's not much point to that. It's true I started up a little company to manufacture a chip I designed, but so did a lot of other guys in the Valley."

A *frisson* of recognition rippled through Allegra. Once again she had the vague, haunting sense of knowing something about him that she just couldn't pin down. But that didn't make any sense. She had never had any dealings with small computer firms.

Before she could pursue the matter, Simon gestured toward the window. "We're leaving."

Allegra leaned forward. She had already seen one launch of the *Silver Zephyr*, but the experience was far too impressive to be ignored.

On radioed commands from the control center, the gangway was rolled away and the entrance sealed; then the mooring lines were loosed one by one until finally the last fell away and the great airship was free to move into its natural element, the sky.

She clenched her hands in her lap, dimly aware that the cacophony of music, tinkling glass and conversation had died away. Not even so blasé a crowd as this could pretend to be immune to the grandeur of what they were witnessing.

Slowly, with none of the sudden surge of a plane, the

Silver Zephyr began to rise. At first the movement was almost imperceptible. Treetops seemed to gradually shrink and the watching crowd of reporters grew smaller.

The silence was eerie.

Somewhere in the bowels of the dirigible pumps were emptying the giant air tanks that served as ballast, lightening the load so that the helium could lift them. Huge propellers were revving up to control their direction, but those in the observation lounge had no sense of that. It was as though a great hand were raising them gently toward the heavens.

"Incredible," Simon breathed softly. "I tried to imagine what this would be like, but I didn't come close."

"Neither did I the first time," Allegra agreed, suddenly very glad to have someone to share this wonder with. "Several of our people have been up in hot-air balloons, but they say that isn't very similar because there's no sensation of the great size and strength we have. The closest anyone's come to describing it is Tristan Ward, the inventor, who said it was like sky diving, only in reverse."

"I knew it reminded me of something. That's it."

Her eyes widened slightly. "You've gone sky diving?"

He laughed. "In the paratroopers, but we didn't call it that."

So her guess had been right; he was a man who had seen the brutal side of life and carried the memory of it still. A quick glance from beneath her thick lashes was enough to confirm her impression that he was about thirty-five. She did a quick mental calculation and asked, "Vietnam?"

He raised an eyebrow. "Does it still show that clearly?"

"No . . . well, perhaps. But not in the way I think you mean. You just struck me as someone who didn't have a whole lot of illusions. There had to be a reason."

He finished his champagne and regarded her drolly. "Couldn't I just have been unlucky in love or something like that?"

More lightly than she felt, Allegra said, "Maybe at cards, but not love."

"Oh, no?"

She laughed softly. "You don't really expect me to pursue that, do you?"

"I suppose not." He sighed exaggeratedly. "Still, you can't blame a man for hoping."

"Trying."

"What?"

"The expression: You can't blame a man for trying."

Far in the depths of his eyes she saw a light that made her tremble. "That, too."

"I think," she murmured shakily, "we should go in to dinner." As she said the words a sudden doubt hit her. She wanted to stay with Simon, there was no point trying to kid herself about that. But she had to sit at the captain's table, which was by invitation only.

As it turned out, she needn't have worried. They had

barely entered the ornate restaurant, which might have been lifted intact from Versailles, when the maître d' hurried over to welcome them.

"Ms. Whitney, a pleasure to see you. Everything is perfect. No problems."

"I never doubted it, Henri. May I introduce Mr. York? I'm . . . uh . . . not sure where he's sitting."

A funny thing happened to Henri as he learned the identity of her companion. His already deferential manner became even more respectful. "Mr. York, of course. Welcome, sir. If I may show you both to the captain's table . . ."

Allegra managed rather adroitly to hide her surprise. It didn't do in her business to admit she had been caught off guard. Still, she couldn't resist throwing Simon a perturbed glance, which he returned with a guileless smile.

Winston was already on the scene as they arrived, looking resigned to his fate as he chatted with a senator, the anchor man of a network news show and a rock star whose latest album was at the top of the charts.

His gracious welcome only hinted at the relief she knew he must be feeling now that she was there to take some of the burden off his stalwart shoulders. He introduced her to the other guests rather grandly. "May I present Ms. Allegra Whitney, whose public relations firm has done such an outstanding job of bringing the *Silver Zephyr* to the public's attention."

"Winston and I have something of a mutual admiration society going," she teased. "We're very lucky to have him as captain."

Turning to Simon, she introduced him to the rest of the group. As she did so she watched for signs of recognition, but there were none. More than ever she wondered how he came to be sitting with a group that was in effect the elite of the elite.

Drawing up the list for the captain's table had been her responsibility, and she knew his name hadn't been on it. But Henri was not likely to make such a mistake, and there was a place set for Simon. That meant he had been added after the list left her office, but by whom?

It was hardly an issue she could bring up right then, but she was determined to solve the puzzle before much longer. Simon was interesting enough without also being mysterious.

As they settled down around the table and the usual dinner conversation began, she caught him gazing at her. He looked well aware of her puzzlement and amused by it.

Allegra's mouth tightened. He was a compelling man, and she wasn't about to deny her attraction to him. Though they had known each other only a few hours, she already sensed that all her well established defenses would be of little use if he really made up his mind to seduce her. But neither was she going to let him come much closer than he already had without first getting at least a few of her questions answered.

Or so she told herself as she picked up the menu and studiously tried to ignore the tantalizing scrutiny of his pewter eyes.

Chapter 3

JUST AS SHE HAD EXPECTED, SIMON PROVED TO BE AN undeniably charming and pleasant dinner companion. In conversation he was both witty and erudite. His manners were impeccable, but without any sense of being at all forced. He showed an off-handed familiarity with the far-flung corners of the earth that fascinated her.

Perhaps most notable was the fact that in the midst of a collection of people who seemed intent on impressing each other with their own importance, he was utterly relaxed and unassuming. He seemed a man completely at ease with himself.

Not that he was in any way arrogant. He didn't need to be, not when he possessed so deeply rooted a sense of his own worth. There was only one way Allegra knew of for anyone to acquire such confidence: to possess great wealth and power, and to understand both the privilege and responsibility of that position.

But if that was Simon's background, the fact that they had never met before became even more puzzling. In an effort to solve the mystery she tried to ferret out the details of his life, without success. Her every attempt was discreetly blocked. By the end of the evening she knew nothing more about him than what he had revealed over drinks in the lounge.

Which was why, she told herself, she accepted his invitation to stroll on the enclosed deck after the others adjourned for after-dinner drinks. Perhaps, alone with him, she would be able to get him to open up more and satisfy the curiosity that was increasing with every moment she spent in his company.

"That's quite a group we have on board," she said as they began the circuit. "Have you met many of them before?"

His teeth flashed whitely in the indirect lighting. "No, I don't believe I have. But you seem on a first-name basis with most of them."

She shrugged that off, determined that this time he would not turn the conversation back to herself or some neutral topic, as he had done all evening. "In my business you tend to see the same people over and over. It's inevitable that you get friendly with them. I suppose that's why I'm a little surprised at never having met you before."

"Only a little?"

Despite the teasing caress of his voice, or perhaps

because of it, she was flustered. Gathering all her self-possession, she smiled ingenuously. "Am I being too nosy?"

"No, not at all. I find your interest very . . . flattering."

"As I said, it's part of my business."

They had reached a part of the deck well removed from the crowd streaming out of the restaurant and making its way to the various entertainments arranged for the evening.

Amid the shadowy recesses of stacked deck chairs and tarpaulin-covered mounds of sports equipment, it was very quiet. Allegra's heart began to hammer painfully against her ribs as Simon stopped and gently drew her close to him.

"So your only interest in me is professional?"

"I didn't say that. I mean . . ."

He laughed softly, his lips just brushing her cheek. "Poor Allegra. You're not used to being confused, are you?"

"No," she acknowledged raggedly, not wanting to admit how much she liked the touch of his hands holding her upper arms, or the steely warmth of his body not even the layers of their clothes could mask.

"Neither am I." The taunting humor she had glimpsed abruptly vanished. In his seriousness he was even more compelling. She stared, fascinated, at the firm line of his sensuous mouth as his head slowly bent to her.

At five feet, eight inches in moderate heels, with a lithe, resilient body, she had never thought of herself as small or delicate. But Simon made her feel both.

His massive shoulders blotted out the light spilling from the deck-side cabins even as the overwhelming impact of his virility blotted out all thought. Deep in her throat she moaned softly, a sound of mingled pleasure and dismay he caught in his mouth as he claimed hers.

Allegra stiffened instinctively, but could not maintain it. Her body seemed to have a will of its own, at least where Simon was concerned. Despite her best efforts she became soft and pliant as he molded her to his far larger and more powerful form.

It's only a kiss, she recited to herself over and over, more and more frantically. She had been kissed more times than she could possibly remember. It was no big deal.

Or was it? With Simon, none of her accustomed self-control and inner restraint seemed to work. He demanded everything; without thinking she gave it.

Gently his tongue outlined the inner softness of her lips, tracing the ridge of her teeth before making playful forays within. If he had been in the least rough or inconsiderate she might have stood a chance of denying him the response he so clearly wanted. But his tenderness undid her.

A shiver ran through her as she yielded, her arms twining around the corded column of his throat and her tongue meeting his in a sensual feint and parry that left her breathless with need.

The physical pleasure she found with him took a quantum leap upward as she felt his big body tremble in her arms and knew she could move him as effortlessly as he did her.

Something rare and magical was happening between them, chemistry, kismet, whatever. Even her rational mind, which had always laughed at such romantic fantasies, was shocked into silence. Only sheer female instinct was left, and she meant to make the most of it.

Her raised arms had brought her breasts into even closer contact with the hard wall of his chest. She knew he must be able to feel her erect nipples through the thin layers of silk and linen separating them. Very deliberately she brushed herself against him and waited for his response.

He didn't disappoint her. The arms that a moment before had held her so gently tightened inexorably. His big hands slid down her bare back, seeming to savor every centimeter of silky skin before coming at last to her rounded buttocks. Gripping her, he arched her to him, making her vividly aware of his state of arousal.

"Allegra . . ." he groaned thickly, "I didn't realize . . ." He broke off, taking her mouth again with raw passion that, far from dismaying her, only fueled her own already intolerable desire. Long, heated moments passed as they were lost to all the rest of the world, a man and a woman alone in an enchanted land of their own creation.

They were nearing the borderline beyond which it would be impossible to draw back. Both were aware of it, and both knew they could not allow themselves to slip over, at least not in their present surroundings.

Reluctantly Simon raised his head and smiled down at her. His pewter eyes were somnolent with desire. He laughed huskily. "You should be posted with danger signs. Nothing I've ever touched has been so intoxicating . . . or so explosive.''

"I know what you mean," she admitted candidly. The time for playing games with this man was long past, if it had ever been. "I've never felt anything like this. It's . . . terrifying.''

Without letting her go, he tilted her chin up and gazed at her quizzically. "That's an interesting choice of words. Why should you be frightened of what's happening between us?''

"Because you're a stranger and I . . .''

"You don't like strangers?''

"It isn't that. I've always been very . . . careful.''

"Yes," he murmured slowly, his thumb caressing the smooth curve of her chin. "I can see how you would have had to be, to have accomplished so much in such a short time.''

"Actually, my associates think of me as quite a risk-taker.''

"In business, but not in your personal life. That's true, isn't it, Allegra?''

It unnerved her to realize how thoroughly he understood her. That didn't seem fair, not while he was still such a mystery. Driven to bridge that gap between them, she said slowly, "You seem so different from me, so impervious to the confusion I'm feeling. At dinner I was thinking that you must be very wealthy and influential. It's the only explanation I could come up with for the effortless air of confidence you project.''

She had gone too fast, inadvertently treading on

some very sensitive part of his psyche. His arms abruptly dropped away from her as his expression became hooded. "Does it matter to you whether or not I have money?"

Allegra couldn't help it; his defensive glare made her laugh. In a way she hated to puncture his righteous anger; it was the strongest emotion other than plain old lust that he had shown so far. But she couldn't resist putting a sharp pin to that particular balloon. "Simon, if you didn't have money, you wouldn't be here. This isn't exactly a charity cruise."

He stared at her a moment, clearly taken aback by her straightforward logic, before grinning ruefully. Falling in with her gentle mockery, he said, "Maybe I'm having one mad fling before declaring bankruptcy."

"And maybe I'm Little Miss Muffit. Somehow, you don't strike me as the failure type."

"Oh, no? What type do I strike you as?"

"If you're looking for flattery . . ."

"Perish the thought. Tell you what, I'll go first and tell you how you seem to me. Then we'll trade places. Okay?"

"Seems fair enough." In sharp contrast to her jaunty tone, she unconsciously bit her lower lip as she waited to hear what he would say.

"Don't do that." He leaned forward, touching his mouth to hers, soothing away the tiny, self-inflicted hurt. Before she could react he straightened again and regarded her wryly. "Maybe we'd better keep some distance between us or we'll never get any talking done."

"Is this enough?" she teased, moving back all of half-a-dozen inches.

"Plenty," he assured her, straight-faced. "Now, where was I?"

"You were about to list all my virtues."

"Lord, I hope not! Virtue's a wonderful thing in a woman, provided it isn't carried to extremes. Let's concentrate instead on your more worldly qualities."

A ripple of anticipation raced through her as his gaze moved leisurely from her slightly flushed face down the full length of her body before repeating the same path back up. Huskily he murmured, "You're a beautiful woman, Allegra. But that can't be any news to you."

"You think not? The whole time I was a teenager my nickname was 'Beanstalk.' That's not likely to instill great confidence in one's womanly charms."

"Maybe not, but you sure grew out of it. I've yet to see a beanstalk with curves like yours."

"Have you seen many?"

"Many what?"

"Beanstalks. I thought maybe you were a farmer."

He shook his head good-naturedly at her teasing. "We'll get to me. I'm not finished with you yet. Let's see . . . where was I? Oh, yes, beautiful. And intelligent. That's obvious, or you would never have accomplished what you have. The combination of brains and beauty isn't as rare as some people seem to think, but it's still unusual enough to deserve comment."

Allegra was impatient to get on to him. In his easy mood, she hoped to get at least some of her questions answered. "Anything else?"

"Yes. You have a great deal of inner strength.

You're used to depending strictly on yourself. Though
you look as if you were born with a silver spoon in your
mouth, my guess is you were anything but. You've
worked damn hard to get where you are, and I'll bet
you haven't allowed yourself many distractions along
the way.''

He paused a moment, as though making one final
assessment, before he nodded firmly. ''You've never
been married, and while you date frequently, it's more
often than not associated with business. There's no
special man in your life, nor are you looking for one.
You told the truth when you said what was happening
between us was terrifying. Part of you is tempted to put
as much distance between us as you possibly can. But
the other, I hope stronger, part wants to brave the fire
and discover what we might have together.''

Allegra became aware that her mouth had dropped
open. She closed it firmly and took a deep breath.
Rather shakily, she murmured, ''That's remarkable.
Are you sure you don't do this for a living?''

''As a matter of fact,'' he teased, ''I have a
reputation for not being good with people. Because
I've spent almost all my time recently with computers,
it's taken for granted that I'm pretty insensitive.''

''I never take anything for granted.''

''Good policy.''

''My turn now?''

He grinned crookedly. ''I could go on, but we'd be
here all night. Shoot.''

Allegra smiled. She was going to enjoy this. ''You,
Simon York, are very mysterious. Now don't get that
innocent look, it won't work with me. You climb out of

a vintage car that someone has lovingly restored, introduce yourself to the first woman who catches your eye and clamber on board a dirigible without a blink, all the while dressed in jeans from Sears and a white button-down shirt from Brooks Brothers. You're on the list for the captain's table—a list, incidentally, which I made up—yet no one seems to know you. You're obviously educated, cultured and successful, even if you do try to pass yourself off as just another computer jockey. What's more, you make my antennae twitch.''

She frowned at him sternly. ''Don't you dare laugh. Over the years I've learned to trust my instincts. Right now, they are positively shouting at me that you are here for something other than just a good time. So how about telling me what it is?''

''And you wondered if *I* do this professionally . . .''

''You're trying to change the subject back to me. It won't work.''

''All right, all right. I surrender. I'll tell you the truth.'' Something about the way his eyebrows waggled warned her that he was about to do anything but. His next words confirmed that. ''I am here to meet the woman of my dreams and woo her away from all worldly distractions so that she will agree to spend the rest of her life with me.''

''In your palace by the sea?''

He frowned at her biting tone. ''Why do you say that?''

''It seems to fit, like something out of a poem instead of real life.''

''Poetry and real life aren't mutually exclusive, Allegra. Sometimes they intertwine.''

"Not," she told him flatly, "in my experience."

He shrugged, as though that somehow didn't matter. "Nor mine. But that doesn't mean I've given up dreaming."

The very quiet of his voice was a reprimand. Allegra could feel herself flushing. Why was she trying to pretend to be something she wasn't? The invulnerable career woman facade might do for others, but Simon saw through it instantly.

His gaze reached clear to the vulnerable inner core she so effectively hid from the world, to the woman who longed to be held and touched as she had been only short moments before. And would be again?

Something of her yearning must have shown in her face, for Simon sighed softly. Even as his hands reached for her again, he murmured, "We're going too fast, honey."

"I know," she whispered as she nestled against his chest. Funny how perfectly she fit there, as though the curve of his arms and the hard strength of his body had been made for her. "I know . . . and I don't care."

Without hesitation, she slid her hands up to cup the back of his head and bring his mouth down to hers. All the years of caution and self-discipline dropped away from her as though they had never been. A heady sense of freedom, greater than any she had ever known, coursed through her.

She was Allegra Whitney, twenty-eight-year-old business woman. Successful, respected, even envied. She had more than most people could ever aspire to, and she found a deep sense of satisfaction in her accomplishments.

Or at least she had. Before Simon came to shake her out of her complacency and show her a world she had never before so much as glimpsed. The discovery made her at once exhilarated and resentful. Her existence had been so neat and tidy, and he had shaken it so remorselessly.

But what did that matter when compared with the warmth of his lips against hers, the velvet thrust of his tongue stroking hers, the virile power of his body finding its answer in the moist heat of her loins?

With a shock she realized just how badly she wanted to make love with him, enough to forget the principles of a lifetime and engage in the ultimate act of intimacy with a man she barely knew.

That desire, so alien to herself, stunned her. She was being transformed into someone she could barely recognize and wasn't sure she even liked. Not Allegra Whitney anymore, but Simon York's woman. Dependent on him to make her real when, as he had so astutely guessed, all her life had taught her to depend on no one but herself.

She couldn't do it. Not if she was to have any hope of retaining her self-respect. Other women might be able to engage in casual affairs and, when they were over, go on as if nothing had happened, but not her.

Panic flared through her as she instinctively pressed her hands against his chest at the same moment she tried to wrench her mouth free. Obeying instincts every bit as ancient and demanding, Simon refused to let her go, until the full measure of her fright reached him and he groaned deeply.

"Allegra . . . don't tell me . . ."

"We have to stop, Simon. I won't do this. I can't."

For a terrifying moment she thought he would ignore her protestations. The intensely male flare deep within his eyes told her that he was tempted. They were alone in the secluded section of the deck; everyone else was inside enjoying the cabaret show or dancing. No one would hear her if she cried out for help.

As instantly as the thought occurred to her, it was gone. The taut bleakness stamped on his aquiline features made it clear he was horrified by his brief struggle with his conscience, a struggle which he obviously believed should not even have been necessary.

Dropping his hands as though her skin suddenly burned him through the cool mauve silk, he stepped back hastily. "I'm sorry, Allegra. I don't know what happened. I've never been like this. . . ."

He laughed humorlessly, the sound making her wince. She hurt for the pain she knew he was feeling, and wanted to soothe it, but before she could even attempt to do so he brushed a hand wearily through his hair and said, "There's no excuse for the way I made you feel. Please believe me, it won't happen again."

Remembering the exquisite moments in his arms before her fear had struck, she smiled gently. "I hope that isn't true, Simon. What you made me feel was beautiful. But as you said, we're going awfully fast. We just need to slow down a bit."

He stared at her silently, plumbing the depths of her hazel eyes until he was convinced she meant what she said. Then he smiled ingenuously, with the open relief of a young boy. "Thank you," he murmured huskily.

"I'm not sure I deserve your understanding, but I do appreciate it."

The distant strains of music drifting on the scented air offered them both a welcome distraction. Simon nodded toward the candelabra-lit lounge. "Shall we?"

Allegra nodded. The opportunity to remain in his arms without further committing herself was too good to resist. Tomorrow she would think about the wisdom of letting Simon York get so close to her . . . or perhaps the next day. But for now she was going to put aside the doubts that continued to plague her and give herself up to the magic of his touch.

What was that he had said about continuing to dream even in the face of all life's harsh realities? Perhaps it wouldn't hurt her to do the same. After all, reality seemed to have no part of a fantasy voyage among the clouds, where even the most improbably romantic dreams just might come true.

Chapter 4

LAND WAS ONLY A MEMORY AND THE SEA THE ONLY reality when Allegra awoke the next morning.

She had left the curtains open to reveal the vast expanse of sky and ocean, and had drifted off to starlight and the pale glow of the moon weaving a silvery bridge across the darkling water.

Now the ghostly hues of night were gone, banished by the relentless sun that drenched the world. Thin streams of high cirrus clouds lay against the cerulean infinity, matched by the traces of froth on the cresting waves below.

Standing at the window, she gazed out at the seemingly limitless vista. The horizon was no more than a thin line ineffectually separating two worlds, giving them the appearance of merging until the elements of each became endlessly entwined.

There was no sense of motion, and no sound except the muted whir of the ventilation system and the whisper of her own breath. The filtered air was odorless except for the clean, sleep-warmed scent of her body, so familiar as to be all but unnoticeable.

The tranquility weighed gently on her mind, urging her to return to the wide, soft bed and lose herself once again in sleep. But she resisted the impulse and instead padded naked into the luxuriously appointed bathroom.

As she went through the usual morning ritual of showering and doing her hair and face, she made a halfhearted attempt to avoid thinking about Simon. But even as some stubborn instinct prompted her not to let him dominate her mind, she could not help but remember what had passed between them the night before.

A soft, almost wistful smile curved her mouth, until she caught sight of it in the mirror and frowned. Was that what he was doing to her? Turning her into some cow-eyed creature devoid of even the remnants of sense?

Harsh judgment, perhaps, but under the circumstances it might be as well to be a little tough on herself. All too easily she remembered the pleasure she had found in his arms, the delicious sense of yielding to his strength and virility spurred by the tremulous conviction that he would never harm her.

An unladylike snort bounced off the marble walls of the bath. She had nothing whatsoever to base that belief on except hormones, and she was damned if she was going to let her glands rule her life. They never had before, and this was hardly the time to start.

So Simon was a devastatingly attractive man who

woke her to yearnings buried deep within her. So
what? She had dealt with men like him before. Charming, witty, sexy . . . not to forget compelling, funny,
sexy . . . and then of course there was intelligent,
strong, sexy . . .

She groaned in irritation and stepped out of the
shower, toweling herself off with rather more vigor
than was absolutely necessary. All right, so she had
never actually encountered anyone like Simon before.
That didn't mean she couldn't cope with him. If she
just kept her head on straight, everything would be
fine.

Feeling better about herself now that she had made
up her mind not to act like a love-stricken schoolgirl,
she began applying a moisturizer to her skin as she
hummed softly. A moment later she broke off and
glared into the mirror. The song drifting through her
head was one which the string quartet had played last
night as she and Simon danced under the stars.

It had been well past midnight when he brought her
back to her cabin, pausing at the door to touch a gentle,
undemanding kiss to her upturned lips. "Sleep well,
Allegra," he had murmured huskily before vanishing
down the corridor, leaving her feeling curiously bereft
and disappointed.

Not that she had wanted him to stay, exactly. She
had wanted . . . what? That time could somehow be
speeded up and the difficult, getting-to-know-you inter-
val be cut short. A fanciful urge, not at all the sort of
thing she was given to. But real nonetheless.

Dawn had been less than an hour away when she

finally fell into an uneasy sleep filled with dreams of Simon that made her blush even to remember them. Curiously enough, for all her lack of rest she woke feeling invigorated and more than ready to face the new day. Her first full day with Simon.

Shaking her head wryly at her own sentimentality, she hastily completed her makeup and slipped into a pair of taupe linen slacks and an off-white cotton knit top. The outfit was at once suitably casual for her surroundings yet elegant enough to discreetly proclaim her right to be there.

The coffee on the silver breakfast tray she had ordered was still steaming. She took a final sip before leaving her room. Outside in the corridor it was very quiet. Many of the cabins had "Do Not Disturb" signs hanging from the doors.

After the partying that had gone on the night before that was hardly surprising. She guessed most of the passengers wouldn't appear until noon, when there would be a great demand for Bloody Marys and other restoratives. All the better, since she wanted to take a quiet look around the *Silver Zephyr* and see how everything was holding up.

A steward was vacuuming the ornately carved staircase linking the decks. He returned her smile and nodded courteously. Other stewards were hard at work dusting the gilt wall sconces, polishing the plate glass windows and setting out crystal vases of fresh flowers.

Observing the busy scene, Allegra thought back to the debate that had waged over the interior design of the dirigible. One faction had held out for a starkly

modern "Space Age" decor, while another had insisted on recreating the glamour of the great liners that
had once plied the North Atlantic in the age before jets.

It had fallen to her to settle the dispute in the most
effective way possible, by drawing up two different
advertising brochures, one for each design approach,
and letting the backers see for themselves how much
more effective the nostalgic look was than what she
privately referred to as "Early Technocrat."

As the project progressed that turned out to be only
one of many contributions she made, with the result
that she now thought of the *Silver Zephyr* as very much
her own, a feeling she knew Winston and all the rest of
the crew shared. They took great pride in what they
were doing and what it might mean for the future of
transportation worldwide.

But before any such grandiose expectations could be
realized, they had to get through their maiden voyage.
Reminding herself of that, Allegra headed toward the
purser's office to check on how everything was going.

Kirsten Ludlow was already at her desk, looking
completely in control despite the early hour. She
smiled a welcome and nodded toward the coffee pot.
"How about a cup? It's fresh."

Of course. Kirsten would never tolerate stale coffee
any more than she would put up with snagged carpet-
ing, rude waiters, sloppy service, or any other of the
small, myriad deficiencies that could add up to disaster.
That was what made her such an effective watchdog of
the passengers' comfort and welfare.

At forty-two, with twenty years at sea behind her,
she had been an eminently logical choice for purser of

the *Silver Zephyr*. Kirsten spoke seven languages fluently, had traveled all over the world, was a licensed paramedic, and could in a pinch put out fires and fly airplanes.

She was also highly attractive in a coolly blond way that owed nothing to artifice. Her honey-hued hair was as natural as the laugh-lines around her light blue eyes and generous mouth. In the months they had worked together to ready the *Silver Zephyr,* she and Allegra had become good friends.

"How does it look to you so far?" Kirsten asked as Allegra settled into the chair beside her desk.

"No problems that I can see. Everyone seems to be having a good time. What do you think?"

"Definitely. We've even had fewer than the expected number of pet peeves. You know the kind of thing. Someone doesn't like the color of the bath towels, or someone else insists on a special diet we haven't been told about. Considering who we're carrying on this trip, the passengers seem remarkably content."

"Let's just hope they stay that way. We want the word-of-mouth advertising to be great."

"It will be," Kirsten assured her. "You've laid the groundwork perfectly. Now just sit back and enjoy the results."

Allegra laughed softly. "I wish it were that simple. But I do have to agree that so far everything seems to be going well. There were just one or two things I wanted to ask you about."

"Sure, go ahead."

"Well, to start with, there was a man sitting at the

captain's table last night whom I don't remember putting on the list. He must have been added later, since Henri knew about him. So I just wondered what the story was.''

"Hmmm . . . would that be Simon York?''

Allegra nodded with what she hoped was appropriately mild interest and sipped her coffee.

"I got a call from Tristan's office about that. Mr. York is a friend or associate of his. I'm not sure exactly. But he did make it clear he wanted him to have the best of everything.'' The purser frowned thoughtfully. "I hope I didn't make a mistake putting him on the list, but with Tristan's okay—''

"No, not at all,'' Allegra assured her hastily, hoping that her surprise didn't show. Simon knew Tristan? They were close enough for Tristan to make a special effort to roll out the red carpet for him? Then why hadn't Simon said anything about that when she mentioned Tristan's name the night before?

Her smile did not quite reach her eyes as she set down her coffee cup and rose. "I don't want to keep you from your work, so I'd better get going.''

"There's no need to rush. What was the other thing?''

Allegra frowned, unsure what her friend meant. "Other?''

"You said there were one or two things on your mind.''

"Oh . . . well, actually there was only this business with Mr. York. Thanks for clearing that up.''

"My pleasure. If I can help with anything else, just

let me know." Kirsten walked with her to the door. Her thick-fringed eyes that could look as icy as a Scandanavian fjord were warm with humor as she said, "He certainly is a fantastic-looking man. I can't blame you for being interested in him."

Allegra could feel herself blushing. "I'm just doing my job."

Her friend looked at her curiously before she smiled indulgently. "Of course you are."

Despite assurances to the contrary, Allegra left with the decided impression that she had tipped her hand. Fortunately Kirsten was the soul of discretion and could be counted on to keep their exchange to herself.

Which was just as well, since Allegra was getting more steamed by the moment and would not be in any mood to endure the good-natured teasing of her colleagues should they get wind of her attraction to Simon.

The more she thought about how he had deliberately sidestepped her questions, the angrier she got. How amusing he must have found her efforts to draw him out. Keeping her in the dark had been child's play. She had allowed herself to be distracted with such ease that it would be no wonder if he quickly tired of the game.

The color drained from her cheeks as she forced herself to confront the possibility that what had meant so much to her might be nothing more than a passing amusement to him.

Hard on that tormenting thought came wry impatience with her own insecurity. For a woman who had triumphed over immense odds to build her own busi-

ness and make her own way in the world, she was
showing a remarkably timid streak.

Since when did she have so little faith in herself that
she could doubt the soundness of her own judgment?
Since she met Simon, that's when. He shook her to the
very foundation of her being and in the process did
unpleasant things to her self-possession. She was not
sure of anything where he was concerned, but she
needed to be, desperately.

And that meant she had to see him. It couldn't be put
off a moment longer. Steeling herself, she picked up a
courtesy phone and asked to be connected with his
suite.

After half-a-dozen rings she finally accepted the fact
that he wasn't there and hung up. Very few of the
passengers were stirring as yet, and the small number
that were up and about were clustered in the dining
room enjoying breakfast. Simon was not among them.

A brief glimpse of the library turned up nothing,
neither did stops at the observation lounge, exercise
room or masseur. The last, however, was able to give
her a clue.

"Is he a big guy?" Larry Wallicker asked. "About
six-two, brown hair, tanned?"

"That's him."

"He's swimming laps."

Allegra thanked him and made her way to the
Olympic-size pool within a domed enclosure that
provided a magnificent view in all directions. Simon
apparently wasn't interested in examining the beauties
of nature; instead he was providing one himself.

She stopped near the shallow end, watching as he cut cleanly through the water with powerful strokes, the long, pure line of his body causing hardly a ripple. There was no one else around. He had the place entirely to himself, except for her, and as yet he was unaware of her presence.

Giving in to the temptation to leave him in ignorance, if only to prolong her enjoyment of his magnificent form, Allegra sat down on one of the deck chairs and studied him unabashedly.

Sunlight bounced off the corded muscles of his broad back and arms, accentuating the graceful arch of his body as it cleaved the water. He must have been in superb condition to swim so effortlessly.

A memory of the steely arms that had held her the night before rippled through her. She shivered slightly, suddenly cold in her thin cotton sweater. Sharply she reminded herself that she was angry with him.

He completed his last lap and propped himself up against one end of the pool with his body dangling into the water. Shaking his head, he sent a spray of droplets in all directions. As he pushed away the thick lock of chestnut hair that had fallen across his brow and replaced his wire-rim glasses on the bridge of his nose, he saw her.

"Good morning. I didn't realize you were here."

"I know. I didn't want to disturb you."

The laugh lines around his eyes grew more pronounced as he grinned at her. "You've already done that. Did you sleep well?"

"Yes," she informed him tartly. "How about you?"

He shrugged. "No, but then I didn't expect to." His eyes ran over her appreciatively as he observed, "You're up early."

"I had a lot on my mind. Are you planning to stay there all day?"

"Nope, toss me a towel, will you?"

As she did so Simon hoisted himself out of the pool. Streams of water ran off his huge, burnished body, over sculpted muscle and corded sinew, down his broad torso and taut waist, past his lean hips and long, tensile legs.

Allegra swallowed hastily. His chest was covered with a thick mat of glistening curls that tapered in a narrow line along his flat abdomen before disappearing beneath the waistband of the black swim briefs that only slightly exceeded the absolute minimum required for modesty.

Very little was left to her imagination. The vague, half-admitted fantasies she had allowed herself about how he would look unclothed fell far short of the mark. He was magnificently male in all respects, and the woman in her was hard-pressed not to respond.

The knowing glint in his eye told her that he was well aware of her preoccupation and was amused by it. That alone was enough to stiffen her spine and remind her of why she had gone looking for him.

Without preamble, she demanded, "Why didn't you tell me you knew Tristan Ward?"

Simon didn't answer at once. Instead he finished drying himself, pulled on a white knit shirt and slipped his feet into sandals. The sight of him going about those ordinary tasks with such innate grace distracted

Allegra. She couldn't manage to get impatient with the delay.

At length he said, "I meant to tell you; there just hasn't been an opportunity."

"How about last night, when I first mentioned him?"

"It was a little too early in our acquaintance to be blurting out my association with Tristan. You see, I would prefer to keep that under wraps for the duration of this trip."

The door to the pool area opened and a short, bleary-eyed man entered. He murmured a good morning and proceeded to strip off his robe before lowering his plump body into the water with an audible groan.

"Let's go out on deck," Simon suggested.

Allegra managed to restrain her curiosity until they reached a secluded spot where they couldn't be overheard. But once there, she wasted no more time. "Are you here in Tristan's place, as some sort of observer?" She had almost said spy, but caught herself. There was no sense antagonizing Simon, not when so much remained to be learned about him.

"More or less. Tristan thought that as long as he couldn't make the trip himself, he might as well send someone who didn't have a stake in the venture and would therefore report back objectively."

"Doesn't he trust the rest of us?"

"I wouldn't say that. He just understands how deeply involved you are in this project, as he is himself. That's bound to affect your perceptions. He'll get a different point of view from me, which is what he wants."

"I see . . . I think. But how did he happen to pick you for the job?"

Simon shrugged. Leaning against the railing, he said, "Tristan and I have been friends a long time. We fought together in Vietnam, and we've been partners in a couple of business ventures. We've helped each other out before, so I guess it was just logical for him to call me."

Allegra studied him carefully. She sensed something beneath his words that she couldn't quite put her finger on. His explanation for how he came to be on board and what he was supposed to do there just didn't ring true. There was an underlying current of evasion that disturbed her. It was as though he were telling her part of the story, but not all.

"How fortunate," she murmured, "that you were able to get away on such short notice. I presume it was short? After all, until a few hours before launch we thought Tristan would be on board."

"He called me from the hospital when he realized he'd be laid up awhile. Fortunately I'd just concluded a business deal, and that left me with some time on my hands, so it worked out perfectly."

Allegra badly wanted to believe him. Tristan had a low tolerance for both fools and frauds. If Simon was his friend, then he must be every bit as intelligent and trustworthy as he seemed.

That should mean that it would be safe for her to follow her instincts where he was concerned. But she couldn't ignore the fact that, however he dressed it up, he had been sent to keep an eye on them all, including her. While she had absolute faith in her ability to do her job, that made their relationship at least semiprofessional.

Early on in her career she had seen ambitious, capable women self-destruct because they didn't know how to separate their personal and professional lives. Allegra had promised herself never to fall into the same trap, and so far she had avoided it adroitly.

But no man had ever tempted her as Simon did. He made her feel more alive than she ever had before, and he made the world seem a wondrous place of limitless possibilities.

Last night, when he had escorted her back to her cabin, she had been on the verge of forgetting all her most closely held principles and asking him to stay. Now she was glad she had not. At least she still had the option to withdraw if she chose.

A wry smile touched her eyes as she thought of that. All the time she was considering what he had told her, her gaze had been drawn irresistibly to him. Her mind might be determined to weigh the situation unemotionally, but her body had far different ideas.

Just being close to him made her mouth go dry and her stomach tighten. She wanted to be in his arms, to feel the gentle persuasion of his lips on hers and know the virile power of his body against her far softer form.

But she also wanted to be safe. Simon represented enormous risks that could upset not only the equilibrium of her heart, but also the hard-won success of her business.

She was more determined than ever to go slowly with him, even as she realized with painful clarity just how very difficult that was going to be.

Chapter 5

PERHAPS SIMON SENSED SOMETHING OF HER UNEASE, for he made no demands on her over the next few days. As the *Silver Zephyr* completed its Atlantic crossing and neared the coast of Ireland, Allegra could look back on delightful hours spent in the company of a man who seemed determined to woo her as gently and carefully as if he were a knight of old and she a noble maiden.

Such storybook images amused her even as she could not help but find them apt. In their luxurious surroundings, cut off from all the rest of the world, they might have been on another plane of existence, where none of the usual rules applied and anything was likely to happen.

There was a sense of enchantment about the voyage that affected even the most jaded and blasé. Men and women to whom pretension was second nature were beginning to relax most disarmingly. Steely-eyed tycoons, social butterflies and media celebrities were all turning into real people.

Even the time-honored tradition of never allowing oneself to be impressed by anything was giving way to an almost childlike pleasure in the wonders unfolding before them.

On the second day out, when a school of whales was spotted, the observation deck was mobbed by eager viewers. Sunsets were avidly watched, as were sunrises, though with somewhat lower attendance. As the crossing neared its end an informal competition sprang up to see who would be the first to spot land.

A British racing car driver won by a hair's breadth over an Italian tenor as the patchwork quilt of Ireland emerged out of the misty morning. By afternoon they had passed over the Kerry peninsula and were heading east toward their mooring just outside Dublin.

The Shannon River was a glittering ribbon beneath them as they followed its winding course toward the capital. All along their route, crowds had gathered to welcome the great airship.

Under Winston's careful guidance they were able to fly low enough to see the faces of the men, women and children who waved at them. Allegra was surprised and deeply touched by their reception. It seemed that even in this day, when people had lost their sense of the marvelous, they had managed to light a spark of adventure in the most land-bound hearts.

As the verdant land of Tipperary unfolded beneath them Simon said quietly, ''My grandfather came from here. I've always meant to come back, but this is the first chance I've had.''

Allegra looked at him in surprise. "My mother's people came from just across the river in Galway.''

He shot her a teasing smile that made a coil of heat erupt within her. "That must be why we get along so well.''

"Do we?''

"Hadn't you noticed?''

"Well . . . I had thought we were . . . compatible.''

He laughed shortly. "Honey, we're a lot more than that and you know it. All I have to do is touch you to prove exactly what I mean.''

Mindful of the crowd around them, she backed up a pace. "I'll take your word for it.''

He chuckled appreciatively. "Smart woman. If you'd tried to deny it, not all the curious eyes in the world would have saved you.''

Not at all put out by his confidence, which merely matched her own, Allegra couldn't resist the urge to answer him in kind. "Is that a threat or a promise?''

His smile faded as he said softly, "Only a promise, honey. You should know by now that I'd never do anything to hurt or frighten you.''

Allegra's gaze slid away from him. She was uncomfortable with the sincerity of his claim. If he spoke the truth, then she had no reason to fight the desires of her body any longer.

Simon was an intrinsically honest man; she was as certain of that as of anything. But truth was a subjective thing, appearing in different forms to different people. What he might say now in perfect honesty could turn out later to be painfully incorrect.

"Do you have any plans to see Dublin?" she asked in a not very subtle bid to change the subject.

He allowed her to, just as he had several times before in the last couple of days. But she sensed his growing reluctance to avoid the one topic that was uppermost in both their minds, though as yet unvoiced. Inevitably they would have to face their desire to become lovers, but for the moment at least she was glad of another reprieve.

"I certainly don't want to miss it," he said. "The Shelbourne is supposed to have an excellent restaurant. Will you join me there for dinner?"

Allegra nodded, already looking forward to the evening. "I'd love to, and perhaps we could also see something of the city. Just wander about, if you wouldn't mind."

"Not at all. As far as I'm concerned, that's the only way to get acquainted with a new place."

They were smiling at each other in perfect agreement when a discreet cough distracted them. Winston stood nearby, resplendent in his dress uniform, with every silvery hair in place. Beside him, Kirsten made an equally impressive appearance.

Not for the first time Allegra was struck by how good the two of them looked together. The vivacious purser was the perfect foil for Winston's somewhat starchy formality, while he provided a necessary dollop of leavening for her somewhat tumultuous personality.

"If I might draw your attention to the fact that we are

about to moor,'' Winston murmured with just the faintest hint of reproach at their preoccupation.

"The dignitaries will be coming on board in a few minutes,'' Kirsten explained more gently. "We didn't think you and Mr. York would want to miss them.''

"Of course not,'' Simon assured her, giving a smile that somehow managed to be equally effective with both men and women. Even Winston unbent enough to nod cordially.

"I checked the reception area earlier,'' Allegra said. "Everything's in order. Several of the officers will take the welcoming party on a tour before they leave.''

"I believe the Lord Mayor is particularly eager to get a look at us,'' Winston said as they headed toward the main deck, where the visitors would be received. "He's a former RAF fighter pilot and fascinated by anything that flies.''

Harley FitzStephen turned out to be exactly that. Although he was nearing retirement age, the tall, well-built man with the thick head of pure black hair and sparkling blue eyes was as enthusiastic and curious as a young boy. Accompanied by his wife and half a dozen aides, he fairly bounded up the ramp, pumped everyone's hand vigorously and let loose with a barrage of questions.

Allegra was delighted by him, as were Simon and Kirsten. Even Winston proved susceptible to such Gaelic charm. He was fairly beaming as he introduced his lordship to the three backers assembled to meet him.

Lord Harley was already acquainted with Bertrand Levinson, the financial genius behind the *Silver Zeph-*

yr. The two men had played golf in Scotland and regularly fished for salmon in the streams of Connemara. They already had plans to get together that evening to hash over old times.

Charlie Fletcher, the big, trumpet-voiced engineer who had helped push through the idea for the dirigible despite all the problems and setbacks, also greeted the mayor warmly. It turned out that they had a mutual friend at the Bank of England who had brought them together on several deals.

Only Arthur Rutherford was unknown—except by name—to his lordship, which was hardly surprising considering that the film mogul rarely ventured far from Los Angeles, where his studio and theater empire were headquartered.

Rutherford was something of an enigma to Allegra. She knew he was reputed to be immensely wealthy and to be involved in a host of business ventures, some even stranger than the *Silver Zephyr*. But he was also an intensely private man who had little to say for himself and who was as much a mystery to his long-term associates as to those meeting him for the first time.

Allegra couldn't exactly say that she didn't like him, but he did make her uneasy, a feeling that was accentuated by the fact that Simon also seemed wary of him.

With the introductions out of the way, and the dignitaries proceeding on their tour of the airship, she and Simon were free to leave. "How about getting in a little sightseeing," he suggested, "before coming back here to change for dinner?"

"Sounds good to me. Just let me get my purse."

She was on the way down to her cabin when a junior officer stopped her with news of a transatlantic call coming into the communications room. "It's Mr. Ward, ma'am. He'd like to have a word with you."

That was one summons she could not ignore. "All right. But would you please go up to the main deck and find Mr. York? He's waiting for me, and I'd like him to know I'll be slightly delayed."

As the young man went off on his errand Allegra climbed the stairs to the communications room. Set on the uppermost level of the airship, adjacent to the bridge, it was one of the few areas with no view.

Instead of windows, every inch of wall space was lined with state-of-the-art radio, radar, sonar and computer equipment, all constantly monitored by methodical men and women who counted it a matter of pride to never miss the faintest murmuring from the great beyond that might have the slightest impact on their vessel.

Allegra entered rather gingerly, glancing around until she found the officer in charge of what was referred to as "passenger-access remote communication."

"Mr. Ward is on line two, ma'am," the young woman informed her. "If you'll just take a seat, I'll connect you."

Moments later Tristan's voice reached her clearly over the distance of three thousand miles. "Allegra? Sorry for the interruption, but I thought we should have a chat."

"Don't apologize. I'm always delighted to hear from you. How are you feeling?"

"All right, I suppose. I'm hoping to get out of here within a couple of days."

"You're not rushing it, are you? From what I've heard that was quite a clonk on the head you took. You certainly sound better. When we spoke right afterward you sounded pretty woozy."

"That's how I felt. But I'm not going to get any better lying around here, so the sooner I get out, the better." Grumbling, he added, "This place gives a whole new dimension to boring."

"Poor Tristan. Aren't there any pretty nurses to keep you entertained?"

He laughed at her gentle teasing, but she thought she detected a strained note in his voice that worried her. "Several, but somehow they don't seem to do the trick. Maybe that's because none of them are as good looking as you."

Allegra let the compliment waft over her without a thought. She and Tristan had known each other long enough to establish that they were destined to be nothing more than friends. Their relationship was founded on mutual respect and genuine affection, which suited them both fine.

"Flatterer. Did you just call to soothe my ego or would you like a report on how we're doing?" Before he could answer, she went on, "I can give it to you short and sweet. Everything is great. Smooth as silk. In fact, this may go down as one of the great trouble-free cruises of all time."

"That's good to hear," Tristan said, and this time she was certain of his unexpected somberness. "I just hope it continues."

"There's no reason why it shouldn't."

"Actually . . . there may be. That's why I'm calling."

Allegra's fingers tightened around the phone. Tristan was an eminently sensible man, never given to unfounded concerns. If he was worried, she had every reason to be, too.

Glancing over her shoulder to be sure she couldn't be overheard, she said softly, "What's wrong, Tristan?"

"I'm not sure; that's the problem. There may be nothing."

"Then why are you concerned?"

"Because I've received a warning, anonymously, to the effect that the *Silver Zephyr* will be sabotaged on its maiden voyage. I've talked with the authorities about it, and everyone agrees that it's probably just a sick joke. If I thought otherwise I'd notify the rest of the backers at once and move to curtail the trip. But as it is I thought I should at least alert you to the possibility that everything may suddenly have to be cut short."

"All right, I can understand that. Does Winston know?"

"I spoke with him earlier this morning and told him then that I'd discuss it with you the moment you were free. Notice I said 'discuss,' not just tell you about it. I want your recommendations."

Allegra thought very carefully before she spoke again. No one had to explain to her how much might be riding on the decision Tristan made. Slowly she said, "Without knowing more about the precise nature of the warning, it's difficult to say. But if both you and the authorities believe there's nothing to it, then I think we should go on. To do otherwise would be to sabotage the project ourselves."

"That's exactly what I think. The letter I got was very unclear. No demands were made, no specifics given. Just a blanket warning that the *Silver Zephyr* was in danger. On that basis, I can't justify taking any drastic action."

"I agree. We both know what would happen if the passengers were suddenly told the trip was over. The media would have a field day, and we'd be through before we had barely begun."

Closing her eyes for a moment against the glare of a computer screen, she added, "Tristan, there is one matter I'd like to get straightened out immediately. Where does Simon York come into all this?"

Silence for a moment, then she thought she heard a soft chuckle. But she must have been mistaken. There was certainly nothing to laugh about in the present situation.

"So you've met Simon, have you? What do you think of him?"

"He's very . . . impressive. Care to tell me what he's doing here?"

"Just keeping his eyes open for me. Simon and I are old friends. We were in 'Nam together."

"I know. He told me about that, and about the two of you being in business together off and on."

"He told you about 'Nam?"

"That's what I just said."

"I'm surprised. Simon doesn't talk about the war. In fact, I can't remember the last time he even told someone he'd been in Southeast Asia."

Allegra bit her lip. She was shaken by the knowledge that Simon had given her a glimpse of himself that he usually withheld, especially in light of the fact that she had several times complained about his reticence. "Was it that bad . . . ?"

"Yes, in a word. Simon and I were in the thick of it for almost two years. We saved each other's lives more times than I can remember, and we got to know each other on a level few people ever approach. I'd trust him with anything."

Including the *Silver Zephyr?* Allegra didn't voice that question, but it was uppermost in her mind as she and Tristan spoke for a few more minutes. They went over the situation again and concurred that any action they might take would be at best inadvisable and at worst disastrous.

When she hung up, after wringing a promise from Tristan that he would take it easy and follow his doctor's instructions, Allegra remained where she was for a few moments, thinking over what she had just learned.

It really wasn't all that surprising that a threat had been made against the dirigible. If the events of recent years had proved anything, it was that the world was full of crazies ready to take advantage of any situation. Most of the time they seemed content to merely sow fear and doubt, but every once in awhile, one of them felt driven to act.

She sighed softly as she realized that deep down inside she was more concerned than she had let on to Tristan. Yet she understood full well that any would-be saboteur would find the *Silver Zephyr* a very difficult target.

Mindful of the half-century-old tragedy that had destroyed the dirigible industry, every possible safety precaution had been taken two and three times over.

Nonflammable helium was the propellant instead of the highly explosive hydrogen relied on by the *Hindenburg*. There were backup systems for the backup systems. Computer scanners constantly monitored the precise state of every piece of machinery on board.

And to guard against even the remotest possibility of error, highly trained specialists watched both the computers and each other twenty-four hours a day.

So far as she could determine, there were only two ways the airship could be seriously endangered: by a bomb or a hijacker. Neither was really worth much consideration, because all passenger luggage had been discreetly checked for explosives and weapons before being allowed on board.

That was why the pearl-handled pistol of a world-renowned couturier now rested in Winston's safe, along with the Sikh dagger of an Oscar-winning actor and, remarkably enough, the brass knuckles of one of rock and roll's top female vocalists.

No matter how carefully she thought about it, she had to agree that Tristan's decision to ignore the warning was correct. Yet she still couldn't shake the vague feeling of unease that accompanied her as she left the communications room.

The young officer who had gone looking for Simon was just returning. He tipped his hat courteously as he said, "I'm sorry, Ms. Whitney, but I didn't have any luck finding Mr. York. Seems he left the main deck just a few minutes after you did."

"Oh . . . well, thanks just the same. I'm sure I'll catch up with him."

After stopping by her cabin to finally pick up her purse, she went in search of Simon. As the young officer had said, he was not on the main deck, nor was there any sign of him at the bottom of the ramp.

Vaguely annoyed that he should have gone off and left her without a word, she waited around for a few minutes before deciding to check his suite. She was on her way down there when an announcement came over the loudspeaker.

"Will Mr. White please come to the engine deck, aft compartment."

Allegra froze. Those calmly uttered words were the code phrase alerting the crew to the presence of a fire on board. Forcing herself to nod politely at the middle-aged man and woman walking past her, she waited until they were just out of sight before racing down the corridor toward one of the emergency staircases.

Moments later she was on the engine deck, observing a scene so ordered and precise that it might have been a drill except for the smoky smudges on the once pristine uniforms of the officers and the relieved looks not all their training and discipline could hide.

Stopping one of them, she demanded, "What happened?"

"Just a drill, ma'am. Passengers are not permitted on this level."

"It's all right, Stephens," Winston intervened. "Ms. Whitney is one of us. Not to worry, Allegra. It's all under control."

"What was 'it'?"

"A smallish fire near one of the engine thrusters. Fortunately Kirsten was making one of her periodic inspections at the time and spotted it." An unexpectedly warm smile lit his face as he said, "She's absolutely remarkable, that woman. Grabbed an extinguisher and put it out in no time flat, with Mr. York's help, of course. If it hadn't been for their prompt action, we might still be fighting it."

"Simon was down here?"

"Yes, apparently he wanted to take a look at the engines. Can't say I approve, but he is Tristan's special guest, so I suppose allowances have to be made. Anyway, I can hardly argue with his behavior when he put himself on the line as he did."

Allegra took a deep breath, hoping to steady herself. "Were they really in any danger?"

Before Winston could answer a deep voice from behind her said, "No, of course not. It was just a few sparks."

Turning, she found Simon looking much as he had less than a quarter of an hour before when she had left him on deck, except now his chestnut hair was tousled, ashes stained his burnished skin, and the jacket of his light wool suit was singed.

"Shame about your clothes," Winston said. "We have an excellent tailor on board. Perhaps he can effect repairs."

"It doesn't matter," Simon assured him, his eyes meeting Allegra's. "I'm just glad I was able to help."

"I'll have a full report ready in an hour, sir," Kirsten said as she arrived on the scene and nodded smartly to Winston. Her gray skirt, white blouse and cranberry blazer were darkened by smoke, and her vivid blue eyes were red-rimmed and tearing.

"Nonsense, Purser Ludlow," Winston snapped. "You will report to sickbay at once."

"That really isn't necessary, sir. I'm f—"

"I'll decide what is and is not necessary, Kirsten. Now come along. I want the doctor to check you out immediately." Taking her arm, he gestured to one of the other officers, who hurried over. "Make sure nothing here is disturbed until I return. Also, notify the Lord Mayor's security men of what's happened."

At Allegra's surprised look, he explained, "I don't really think there's any connection between Lord Harley's presence and this incident, but nowadays one never can tell. Just to be on the safe side, we'd better check out the possibility of some IRA-style terrorist action."

"So you don't think it has anything to do with what Tristan . . . ?" She broke off, uncertain as to how much Simon knew about the anonymous warning.

Winston shook his head. "Very doubtful. My guess is it was simply an accident. Sparks from a propeller fan or some such thing. Anyway, we'll find out."

Nodding at her and Simon, the captain took his leave

with an unexpectedly subdued Kirsten in tow. As they headed up the staircase the purser glanced back. Allegra had to cover her mouth hastily to keep from laughing at her friend's broad wink.

Her good humor faded as she turned to Simon. He was watching her warily, as though he understood her doubts and expected her to lash out with them. But Allegra could not. Her disquiet over his presence in the engine compartment at the time of the fire was far outweighed—at least for the moment—by horror at the danger he had been in.

"Are you sure you shouldn't see the doctor, too?" she asked quietly.

He relaxed slightly, but his eyes did not leave her. "There's no need. I'll get cleaned up and then we can go, all right?"

She hesitated only a moment before agreeing. The plain fact was that she wanted to be with him. But that did not mean that she was suspending all her critical faculties in favor of naive faith.

On the contrary. Tristan's warning and Simon's presence at the fire had made her all the more cautious. She was absolutely determined to discover the truth about him before he could hurt either her or the *Silver Zephyr*.

Chapter 6

DESPITE THE STRAIN LEFT OVER FROM THE FIRE, THEIR visit to Dublin was delightful. They wandered through the city, exploring the great avenues that had seen the Republic's fight for freedom early in the century, and the timeless byways that had sheltered O'Casey, Yeats, Synge and others of the English language's greatest writers.

On O'Connell Street they shopped for Belleek china and Waterford crystal, arranging to have everything sent back to the *Silver Zephyr* before going on with their sightseeing. That was one of the principal advantages of an airship: There was no lack of space to store luggage and no concern over weight limits. A good-sized castle could be accommodated in the cargo holds, with room left over.

Dinner was served in a restored Georgian row house along the Liffey River that wound through the city. Allegra had heard that Irish cuisine combined the best of continental traditions with superb ingredients and imaginative flair, and she wasn't disappointed. They feasted on lobster bisque, lamb broiled over a wood fire and chocolate mousse cake washed down by a selection of outstanding wines.

"We'll have to walk this off," Simon said ruefully as they left.

"Or go dancing," she suggested tentatively.

He laughed and shook his head. "You'll have to wait until tomorrow night when we're in London for that. Dublin may well be the only capital in the Western world that rolls up the sidewalks around ten o'clock."

It was true that there were very few people to be seen on the darkened streets, only an occasional late-evening stroller who seemed unconcerned about any of the usual urban crime problems.

"Are we safe walking around like this?" Allegra inquired as they strolled through St. Stephen's Green, pausing to watch the ducks and swans curled up asleep with their heads tucked into their feathers.

"So I've been told. Despite all the political troubles, this place still has one of the lowest crime rates going."

"Maybe even the muggers think there's nothing to come out at night for."

"Now that isn't strictly correct. If you're in the mood for a little music, I know of a place not too far from here."

Allegra was willing enough to give it a try. She liked

the silent, almost ghostly air of the Dublin streets which, despite a recent spate of skyscraper construction, still retained the more gracious aura of an earlier time. But being so completely alone with Simon was undermining her resolve to keep her emotional distance from him. It might be wiser to have some company.

They found that and a bit more. In a tiny nightclub hidden away on a back street more than a hundred laughing, clapping, foot-stomping men and women were gathered for a performance of the Donegal Brothers, fiddle players *par excellence*.

The crowd was international. Irish jostled cheerfully with Germans, Swedes, Japanese, French and Americans. No translations were needed to appreciate the songs which, far from being the usual folk tunes Allegra had expected, turned out to be a haunting melange of traditional music and new works that blended together perfectly.

In the small, densely packed room Allegra and Simon were pushed up against each other. His arm went around her instinctively to protect her from the worst of the press. Tilting back her head, she smiled up at him. "This is terrific. I haven't been in a place like this since I was in college."

"Me, neither, and I seem to remember from those days that I could never get anything better to drink than watery beer or second-rate Scotch. Let's hope they do better here."

They did. A cheerful waiter found them a small table in an alcove, close enough to be part of the fun, but with a precious dollop of privacy. He reappeared moments later with two snifters of a cognac normally available only from the very best wine cellars.

"How did you guess they'd have this?" Allegra asked as she sniffed the amber liquid appreciatively.

"I remember grandfather telling me that the Irish have a fondness for all the best things in life, perhaps because they so rarely experience them."

"Did your family leave here for the usual reason, the poverty?"

"Actually, they had an even better motivation. Grandda' was a Sinn Feiner, one of the lads behind the Easter Week uprising back in '16. The British authorities wanted to 'speak with him,' which generally meant he'd be swinging from the business end of a rope before you could say up the Irish. Grandma was a strong-willed lady. Looked like a puff of wind would blow her over, but had a steel backbone. She packed him, my father and her very pregnant self onto the next freighter bound for Ellis Island."

"Good for her. It sounds as though she had more than a bit in common with Grandmother Alicia Whitney."

"Now that is a very grand sounding name. You surprised me when you said she was from Galway."

"A potato farmer's daughter, when the blight left any to farm, that is. By the time she was sixteen she was sick to death of the poverty and the hopelessness. So when she got the chance to leave, she grabbed it."

"Is that where your ambition comes from?"

Allegra looked at him warily over the rim of her glass. "Perhaps. There's no denying I've got a heavy

dose of it, not that I'd try. I'll never understand why a
trait that's so admirable in a man receives so much
condemnation when it shows up in a woman."

"Because it makes men feel insecure," he told her
matter-of-factly, then smiled as he amended, "Some
men."

But not you, Allegra thought. She doubted even an
earthquake would shake his self-confidence. He would
ride it out just like he seemed to do with everything
else.

"That fire this afternoon really didn't bother you,
did it?"

"Well, it's not something I want to encounter every
day. But there was never any real doubt that Kirsten
and I would be able to get it under control." He
listened to the music for a moment before he asked, "Is
there something going on between her and the captain?"

Despite herself, Allegra giggled. "As incredible as it
sounds, I think there just might be. Winston is acting
very peculiar where she's concerned."

"He's a good man. She could do a lot worse."

"Winston's one in a million," Allegra agreed.
"That's why he was picked to command the *Silver
Zephyr*. It would be great if they made a match."

"You sound like a romantic," he teased gently.

"I suppose I am, although in my everyday life it
would be hard to tell." That was an understatement.
There was no room for romance in her life, and never
had been.

It was a secret source of amazement to her that
someone who could so effectively turn other people's

fantasies into reality seemed to have no need of them herself. At least not until lately. Alone at night in her stateroom she had been having some fantasies that were all too realistic.

Another type of woman might be content with those dreams, but she was not. The strength of character that had already carried her so far in life demanded that she do more than simply wait around for everything to sort itself out. It provoked her into taking a chance.

As the Donegal Brothers struck up another tune and the floor reverberated to the stomping of a hundred pairs of feet, she said, "I spoke with Tristan today, right before the fire. The timing was rather ironic. He told me that he was afraid there might be trouble on board."

Simon stiffened and looked at her in surprise. "He actually said that?"

"Or as good as. He's certainly concerned."

"What sort of trouble?"

"He has no way of knowing. The evidence—if you can even call it that—is very indistinct."

"Tristan doesn't jump at shadows."

"Right now, he doesn't jump at all," she reminded him quietly. "He's counting on you to be his eyes and ears. He trusts you implicitly."

Simon set down his glass and met her gaze unwaveringly. "There's no reason why he shouldn't."

Allegra took a deep breath. She didn't feel ready for a confrontation with him, but neither was she willing to put it off any longer. Taking advantage of the public setting that still managed to afford them some privacy, she said, "Tristan was surprised that you'd told me about being in Vietnam with him, so apparently you are willing to open up to me about your past more than is usual for you. I just wish you'd be as forthcoming about what you're really doing here."

"I told you: I'm here as a favor to Tristan, to give him an objective opinion."

"And is that opinion supposed to include your evaluation of the engine room?"

Instead of answering her directly, he countered with a question of his own. "Why do I get the feeling that you're working real hard at finding reasons to distrust me?"

"That's not true. I'm simply doing my job."

Very deliberately he drew out his arm and glanced at his watch. "It's after five. You're off-duty."

"You know perfectly well that isn't how things work at my level of responsibility. Or do you believe I should simply turn off my brain when I'm with you and simper prettily?" The words came out more harshly than she had intended, but she was stung by his sarcasm and felt driven to retort in kind.

"It might be a refreshing alternative to getting the third degree," Simon snapped. "Hell, Allegra, you're a woman and I'm a man and we happen to be very attracted to each other. However you want to dress it up, that's what it comes down to."

"It doesn't come down to anything unless I say so, and I'm not about to. Not while there's so much about you that doesn't ring true."

Impatiently he drained his glass and glared at her. "What do you want me to tell you? That I'm some kind of crazed saboteur out to destroy my closest friend's life's work? Is that what you really think of me?''

"No, of course not. It's just that—''

"Then why the hell do you keep acting like you do?''

The couple at the table next to them sent them a reprimanding look. He dropped his voice slightly, but did not mask his annoyance. ''You're afraid of something, Allegra, and it's got nothing whatsoever to do with any possible threat to the *Silver Zephyr*. You're running scared, looking for emotional bolt holes to hide in. I'll be damned if I can understand why.''

"Maybe you can't understand because it isn't true," she shot back even as her mind was reeling from the accuracy of his perception. For an engineer who had a reputation for not being good with people, he was remarkably on target in his analysis of her.

Caustically she said, ''Since when did you turn into an amateur shrink? Or do you think you can dissect me the way you would a computer? Take my lid off and you'll find more than you can cope with.''

"I don't doubt it, but that's not the point. You're putting distance between us, and I resent it. I also think it's a terrible waste, considering what we could be sharing.''

If only he weren't so damn smart! He saw through her defenses too easily and made her doubt her own motives. She had to remind herself that she had reason to be wary of Simon, despite everything he said. Her caution did not stem solely from her hesitation about becoming too involved with him too soon. There was more at stake.

"You're talking as though we were the only two people in the world," she pointed out. "As if nothing except our own concerns and needs could touch us in any way. That simply isn't true. We're surrounded by forces we can barely perceive, let alone control."

"And one of those is whatever may be out to sabotage the voyage?"

"Yes."

"All right, then, let's look at this from another point of view: mine. You're suspicious that I may somehow be involved in this unnamed trouble Tristan is worried about." When Allegra opened her mouth to interrupt, he went on brusquely. "You wouldn't have any other reason to question why I was in the engine room, so don't pretend otherwise. You think, however faintly, that I just might be a suspect. Has it occurred to you that works both ways?"

Bewildered, she stared at him. "What does that mean?"

"That I have just as much reason to be suspicious of you as you do of me."

"That doesn't make any sense!"

"Why not? I don't know much about you except that you're a very ambitious woman on the fast track. Maybe you've run into some kind of trouble and are paying off a debt by working for the saboteurs. Or maybe somebody made you an offer that was too good to refuse. Any of that is possible."

"It most certainly is not! You're talking as though I had no ethics, no sense of honor. . . ."

"And that's exactly what you're suggesting about me. It cuts both ways, Allegra. Either we take a chance and trust each other, or we go to our separate corners and come out fighting.''

Her hand shook slightly as she picked up her glass and took a sip. The cognac warmed her from within, giving her the courage to confront what he had just said.

The problem was, everything he claimed was true. If he was as innocent as he implied, then he did have reason to be suspicious of her. Certainly she had far more opportunity to harm the *Silver Zephyr* than almost anyone else on board. Her months of preparation for the voyage had given her an in-depth understanding of how every system and safety feature worked. If she were out to cause trouble, she would know where to start.

Almost to herself, she murmured, ''I'm not normally a distrustful person. Why I should be that way with you is beyond me.''

''It's not so puzzling. We're intensely attracted to each other. No matter what we happen to be saying or doing at any given moment, in the back of our minds we're wondering what it will be like when we go to bed together.''

Allegra laughed huskily. Her anger and hurt were gone, replaced by a far more pleasurable sense of budding excitement. The half-teasing, half-serious gleam in his eyes unleashed a similar response in her. Meeting his gaze, she asked, ''Shouldn't that be 'if,' rather than 'when'?''

He grinned broadly. ''I call them the way I see them.''

They stared at each other for a long moment, silently

telling each other things they weren't yet ready to put into words. Allegra's breath tightened in her chest. The intensity of his gaze was having a very unsettling effect on her equilibrium. She was swept by a rush of heat. Her cheeks flushed as she trembled. Hardly aware that she did so, she put her tongue out to moisten lips that were suddenly dry.

Simon's smoky gray eyes shifted downward to follow the motion. He groaned softly and abruptly stood up, tossing several bills on the table and holding out his hand to her. "Let's go."

Allegra went with him unhesitatingly. It was as though they had been building up to this moment all evening, and now that it was finally upon them, neither wanted to waste an instant.

Outside the warm summer night was tinged with mist drifting off the nearby sea. It wreathed the buildings in feathery tendrils and cast a smoky nimbus around the streetlamps.

Simon's hand was large and warm around her own as they strolled some little distance down the street, finding privacy in the arched entrance of a storefront shuttered for the night.

There he drew her gently into his arms, his touch tentative, as though he were still not absolutely certain how she would respond. Allegra felt no such doubt. She flowed against him as naturally as if he had held her every day of her life.

Instinctively pressing herself even closer, she gave in to the need to return his touch and slid her hands beneath his suit jacket. Through the thin silk of his shirt she explored the hard lines of his back, savoring the contours of powerful muscles and corded sinews.

The hard, tensile strength of his body delighted her. She felt an almost childlike sense of wonder in the differences between them, and in the knowledge that she was the cause of the tremors racing through him. But there was nothing childlike about the languorous smile that curved her mouth as she lifted it to his.

Simon growled deep in his throat. The arms that had been holding her so carefully a moment before abruptly tightened. She was clasped against an unyielding wall of male strength. With fierce tenderness he hungrily accepted all she offered.

The devastating thoroughness of his kiss stunned her. It had not occurred to her that he had been deliberately holding back when he kissed her before, but now she discovered that to have been the case.

Whereas before he had coaxed her with gentle preliminaries, now he staked his claim ardently. His lips parted hers, gaining access for the swift thrust of his tongue that filled her with the taste and texture of him.

He moved slightly, just enough so that she was thrown off balance and had to cling to him. Reaching down, he cupped her derriere through the thin silk dress, running his hands over her repeatedly before he at last squeezed the soft flesh gently as he pressed her against him.

Allegra gasped, the sound smothered by his mouth. His arousal was unmistakable. Deep within she felt

herself turning to liquid heat as her body obeyed the
primeval drive to prepare itself for his possession.

The strength seemed to go out of her legs, leaving
her even more dependent on him to hold her upright.
As their lips clung together, their tongues dueling
ardently, she felt the fierce pounding of his heart and
knew it no more than matched her own.

Far in the back of her mind some remnant of
rationality warned that this was not the place for such
an encounter. Though the street was deserted, there
was no guarantee it would remain so. At any moment
they might find themselves in a highly embarrassing
situation.

Simon must have realized the same, for at length he
raised his head and gazed down at her with undisguised
intent. Thickly he murmured, "We can't stay here.
Let's get back to the ship."

Allegra's silence was her assent. She knew as well
as he did that the time for pretense was ended. They
faced each other honestly, a man and woman ready to
admit their most heartfelt desire. In a gesture that spoke
eloquently of her confidence in him, she placed her
hand in his.

The quick walk back to the *Silver Zephyr*'s mooring passed in a blur. They did not speak or look
at each other again, both realizing that if they did
so, they would be lost. Not until they had been
checked through by the security officer and climbed the
boarding ramp to the main deck did Simon touch her
again.

Raising her hand to his lips, he turned it over and

pressed a gentle kiss to the palm. The exquisite sensation evoked by his caress radiated through her to restore the trembling of her limbs. Her lips parted on a soundless sigh as their eyes met.

"Your cabin?" he asked quietly.

Bravely, she nodded.

Chapter 7

"WHERE'S THE LIGHT SWITCH?"

"Over there . . . down a little . . ."

Their fingers fumbled in the darkness. Simon cursed softly. Despite her nervousness Allegra smiled. It was reassuring to know that he was as wound up as she was.

"There it is . . . just a second . . ."

Light flooded the room, making them both blink. They gazed at each other warily. His eyes glittered with suppressed desire, and the firm line of his mouth was tightly drawn. A pulse beat in the shadowed hollow of his cheek. Allegra swallowed tightly and made a vague gesture toward the small bar built into one wall. "Uh . . . would you like a drink?"

"No . . . but you go ahead."

"I didn't really want . . . that is . . ." She broke off, feeling unaccustomedly awkward and out of her depth. The enormity of what she was doing struck her. How had she come to be alone in her stateroom with a man she had known only a matter of days yet had the clear intention of going to bed with?

Unbidden, the image of how her mother would react to her daughter being in such a situation surfaced in her mind and made her smile.

"What's funny?" Simon asked cautiously.

"Myself. I was just thinking how far from liberated I am."

Some of his tension faded as he smiled back at her. "I'd suspected that."

"Really? I thought I projected the opposite impression."

"We got past impressions awhile ago."

That was true. They were also past pretense, evasion and all the other delaying tactics used by couples not yet sure of what they wanted. Allegra was sure, more so than ever before in her life. For better or worse, she had to share the most intimate experience with him.

They were still standing in the entry hall of the stateroom and, becoming aware of that, grinned at each other wryly.

"In movies it always looks so easy," Simon said.

"In romances it just happens."

He arched an eyebrow. "You read romances?"

"They're my secret addiction. Sometimes I even hide a couple in my briefcase."

"Does that mean I'm supposed to be the square-jawed hero?" He didn't look too confident at the prospect.

"No. It means you're supposed to need me as much as I need you."

That admission reassured him as nothing else could have. He regarded her tenderly. "I need you so much I hurt inside."

Huskily she murmured, "Me, too."

Reaching out a hand, he brushed a finger down the curve of her cheek in a caress that for all its lightness made her feel oddly cherished. "Then maybe we'd better do something about it."

Something, all right. But what? Possibilities flitted through her mind. Should she excuse herself and withdraw to the bathroom to undress? Or was that too forward? Should they just take off their clothes and hop into bed? She didn't think she could manage that.

Silently damning her lack of experience, she waited, wide-eyed and apprehensive, for him to make the next move.

"Allegra," he breathed softly against her hair, "relax. You must know I would never hurt you."

She leaned her head into the protective curve of his shoulder and nodded. "I just feel . . . so clumsy."

Laughter rumbled deep in his chest. "So do I." Tilting her chin up, he met her eyes candidly. "You want to know the truth? I feel like I'm fifteen again and about to lose my virginity."

Startled, she said the first thing that occurred to her. "Wasn't that rather young?"

"Yes, but I'd made up my mind to do it. You see, I'd read somewhere that adolescent boys would be a lot better off if our society didn't keep them in enforced celibacy. Grades would go up, pimples disappear, all that. With those benefits, I figured it was worth taking the plunge.''

"Did you care about the girl?''

"I cared about the whole experience enough not to inflict it on any girl as ignorant—or almost as ignorant —as myself. My carefully-thought-out solution was to turn the whole matter over to a professional.''

"You went to a prostitute?''

"I was seriously considering it,'' he admitted, "when I happened to make the acquaintance of Sadie Webster, a very kind and understanding lady who turned out to be one of the best things that could have happened to me.''

Bending his head, he gently nuzzled the sensitive skin behind her ear as he murmured, "Sadie even warned me that someday I'd meet somebody very special who would knock the stuffing right out of me.'' He laughed dryly. "Bless her, she was right.''

"Have you . . . uh . . . been with very many women?''

"Probably fewer than a lot of men my age. I've never seen the sense of jumping into bed with someone I didn't care about.''

That was good to hear, even if it fell far short of the commitment she hoped for. Selfish to feel that way, though, since she wasn't yet ready to make any long-term promises to Simon. Only to herself. She would hold back nothing from him and do everything possible to create an experience that, whatever happened afterward, they would both treasure forever.

Which still left the problem of how to proceed. Fortunately Simon had some ideas on that score. With what she had already come to think of as his customary decisiveness, he bent and scooped her into his arms.

"I'm too heavy," she protested as he strode toward the bed.

"You feel fine to me. Besides, isn't this what romantic heroes do?"

As a matter of fact, it was. Forgetting her objections, she relaxed and enjoyed what had always been a secret fantasy of hers. Rhett Butler carrying Scarlett up the staircase had nothing on Simon. He even managed to put her down correctly on the bed, so that her hair fanned out over the pillows and her body lay half beneath his.

"God, you're lovely," he breathed as he settled above her, his hands tracing languid patterns along the silken skin of her bare arms. "So soft and feminine. Everything I could want."

Allegra had no choice but to believe him, not when his lips were nibbling so evocatively on the lobe of her ear and his big body was stirring against hers with unmistakable yearning.

A soft moan rippled from her as she reached up under his jacket, stroking his back. "Simon . . . I want . . ."

"Tell me, angel. This has to be perfect for you."

"And you. That's what I want. For it to be perfect . . . both of us . . . together . . ." It was getting very difficult to breathe what with Simon's warm, skillful mouth tracing patterns of fire down her throat to gently push aside the shoulder of her dress and explore the smooth bareness revealed to him.

Even as her own hands were tugging at his shirt,

pulling it loose from his waistband, his were busy at her back finding the zipper of her dress. It gave easily, and she arched upward to let him pull the fabric down over her arms and breasts to her waist.

A blush warmed her cheeks as he stared at her ardently. She wore only a lacy scrap of a bra that hid little from his eyes. Through the sheer fabric the hardened peaks of her nipples could be clearly seen.

The embarrassment she had expected to feel was missing. In its place were only excitement and the certain knowledge that what she was doing was right. Every touch of his hands and mouth, every murmured word of desire and admiration, increased her conviction that they belonged together.

Without hesitation she unfastened his tie and slid it from him before beginning to unbutton his shirt. His skin was warm beneath her touch and lightly roughened by a thick mat of curly hairs.

As her fingers drifted over him he inhaled sharply. "Easy, Allegra. I want this to last."

She did, too, but she still couldn't resist the need to learn his body as he was learning hers. When he slipped her dress completely off, along with her shoes and panty hose, she offered no objection. Instead she urged his jacket from his massive shoulders, then touched a teasing kiss to his mouth before pulling back to unfasten the button of first one cuff and then the other.

The taut set of his features was proof that her untutored efforts at seduction were succeeding beyond even her greatest expectations. Emboldened, she gave in to her fascination and removed his shirt.

For all that he said he was an engineer, presumably with a desk job, he managed to stay in remarkably good condition. He had the lean, hard look of a man accustomed to grueling physical work.

There wasn't an ounce of fat on him. Directly beneath his burnished skin she could feel the steel of hardened muscle and sinew. Through the pelt of curls covering his chest she could make out the thin white line of a scar just below the left nipple. Without pausing to consider the significance of her action, she ran a finger over it lightly.

Simon growled deep in his throat. He seized her hand, drawing it away from him even as he tipped her back onto the bed so that she was lying flat beneath him.

"I'm about ready to explode," he rasped, "and I don't want that. I want to draw this out properly. To give you everything you need."

She meant to tell him that he was already doing that, but somehow she couldn't form the words. They seemed to be lost in the whirling mass of sensation prompted by the touch of his hands on the front clasp of her bra.

It gave easily to his manipulation, falling open to reveal the high, firm mounds swollen with desire. Simon studied her intently, watching for long moments as her taut nipples hardened further.

When he finally could bear the temptation no longer, he filled his hands with her, kneading and squeezing gently until she thought she would go mad from the pleasure he gave her.

Molten rivulets of sensual excitement raced through her, coalescing at the hot, sweet center where she longed to feel him. Her head tossed back and forth on the pillow, her soft, keening murmurs falling like music on his ears.

"That's it, sweetheart. Sing for me. Tell me how much you want this."

"I do . . . oh, Simon, please! Don't torment me."

"It's torture for both of us," he groaned as he bent his head to draw a hardened bud into the moist warmth of his mouth. Rolling it between his lips, he allowed himself a gentle nip that wrung a whimper of delight from her.

As his hands kept up the enticing love play on her breasts, his mouth moved lower, drifting along the satin expanse of her body. Finding the deep indentation of her navel, he tasted it lingeringly before paying homage to the flat plane of her abdomen stretched between the jutting bones of her hips.

Not until the waistband of her silk bikini panties stopped him did he pause and look up again.

Allegra had no doubt of the picture she presented. Her long chestnut hair lay in tangles across the pillows. Her face was flushed, and her eyes glowed. Her moist lips were slightly parted and pouting from the force of his kisses. Her bare breasts rose and fell swiftly with the rapid rate of her breathing. Her nipples were a dark rose and harder than she had ever seen them.

Looking down the length of her nearly naked form, she was vividly aware for the first time of how she must appear to a man of Simon's virility. The attraction—

and purpose—of her womanhood were obvious, as was her desire to have their lovemaking reach its natural conclusion.

Raising her arms with artless grace, she reached out to him. "Please, don't make me wait any longer."

Simon stared at her dazedly for an instant before her entreaty reached him. Sitting up on the edge of the bed, he unsteadily removed his shoes, then rose to slip off the remainder of his clothes.

Allegra watched him frankly. He was so gloriously male that she could not tear her eyes from him. Every inch of taut, burnished skin delighted her. When he returned to the bed and covered her far softer form with his hardness, she gasped in relief.

No further thought of restraint remained between them as his urgent hands slid beneath her panties, cupping her firm behind. Despite the passion raging through him, his touch was gentle as he found the secret, moist part of her and caressed it tenderly.

Allegra bit down on her full lower lip to suppress a cry of pleasure, but could not and had to let it go. The sound exalted Simon. He wasted no time removing the final barrier between them; then he carefully spread her thighs and knelt between them.

"You are so lovely," he muttered hoarsely. "Perfect for me . . ."

With an almost savage groan, he covered her again with his body, capturing her mouth for a soul-wrenching kiss that left her breathless and on fire with the need for more.

Simon denied her nothing. His calloused palms

rubbed repeatedly over her aching breasts as he slid down the length of her body, coming at last to the soft nest of curls sheltering her womanhood.

Divining his attempt, she tried to protest, but was stopped by a shattering caress that pierced her to the very core. Crying out softly, she could only lie submissive under his touch as he drove her to the very edge of ecstasy before suddenly drawing back.

Left suspended on the cusp between arousal so intense as to be painful and fulfillment so exquisite as to be essential, she had no choice but to reach for him.

As her hand closed around him, Simon groaned with the force of his own pleasure. "That's it, sweetheart. Bring me to you. I need you so much. You're everything to me."

"I've never felt like this . . . as though I may die . . . and not care. . . ."

"Paradise can't be any better. You're so beautiful . . . so much a woman. . . ."

"I'm empty inside. . . ."

"Let me fill you, angel. That's it. *Allegra* . . ."

Her name was a hymn to ecstasy, joined by her own cry as they joined together. Simon claimed the place made especially for him with the assurance of a conqueror and the gentleness of a suitor. He made her his with stunning thoroughness even as Allegra took everything he offered with unbridled eagerness.

They moved together in perfect harmony, first slowly, then with increasing wildness until the crest of the wave at last struck them both and carried them far from conscious thought into a realm of the purest rapture.

Through long, timeless moments they hung together at the shimmering peak, full of golden heat that dissolved the barriers between them and forged a bond never to be broken. Descending gradually, they lay together in a tangle of arms and legs as their breathing slowly returned to what could pass for normal.

With a trembling hand Allegra touched his sweat-streaked brow. There was so much she wanted to tell him about the beauty of what they had just shared, so much she saw in his eyes and knew he wanted to express.

But hard on shattering ecstasy came exhaustion more profound than they had ever known. Even as they struggled to stay awake and savor the moment they were falling, still completely together, into the soft cocoon of sleep.

Allegra woke to a dream of sensual delight. Lying on her back on the bed, with her eyes still closed, she smiled languidly. Something was touching the sensitive skin of her inner thighs with feather-light caresses so delicate as to be barely perceptible.

The now-familiar tension began to coil again within her. She stirred seductively, her hips lifting slightly.

A low male laugh of appreciation reached her. Her smile deepened, but her eyes remained closed. She was enjoying her dream far too much to give it up.

Her body was open, vulnerable to the hard, probing touch that moved against it carefully, coming ever closer, entering her very slightly. . . .

Allegra's lashes fluttered. Her breath caught in her

throat as consciousness poured in. Opening her eyes, she met Simon's molten gaze. He gave her a moment to object. When she did not, but instead moved against him in silent accord, he growled deep in his throat and thrust powerfully within her.

In silence, except for their rasping breath, they came again to another throbbing explosion of pleasure, this time even more intense than the first. Allegra was near to fainting with the unbridled force of ecstasy as Simon held her tightly against him, his big body shaking with the strength of his own release.

An eternity passed before they were able to speak. Raising himself on his elbows, Simon gazed down at her tenderly. Under his scrutiny she couldn't help but blush. Laughing indulgently, he dropped a teasing kiss on the tip of her nose.

"You are incredible. This may kill me, but I won't mind at all!"

"Maybe not," she giggled, "but it would be a little hard to explain to the steward." Her breasts brushed against him, and she savored the rough rasp of the hair that lay like a furry pelt over his skin.

Something flickered far back in his eyes, surprise mingled with a look of very male pride. He moved experimentally. "Speaking of hard . . ."

Her eyes widened. *"Again?"*

"I'm afraid so." Grinning unabashedly, he nudged even more deeply within her. "If you wouldn't mind . . ."

Allegra chuckled. His prowess astounded and delighted her. She rightly took it as a testament to the effect she had on him. Winding her arms around his neck, she drew him closer. "It would be my pleasure."

"Oh, I guarantee that," he murmured in the instant before speech became impossible and the night dissolved once again into the incandescent realm only lovers know.

Chapter 8

THE PHONE BESIDE THE BED WAS RINGING. ALLEGRA turned over groggily, reaching out a hand that overshot its goal and knocked the receiver off the hook. It fell with a soft thud onto the thick carpet.

Satisfied that the ringing had stopped, she began to slip back into sleep, only to be disturbed by a persistent drone that evolved gradually into a muted voice.

"Allegra, are you there? It's Winston. I've got to talk with you."

Winston? Oh, *Winston*. Opening her eyes, she searched for the phone, found it and put it to her ear. "Whaz'it?"

"Sorry to wake you, but we've got a problem. I'd like you to come up to my office as soon as possible."

The sober intensity of his voice made sleep fall away as though it had never been. She sat up in bed, drawing the sheet with her, and glanced at the clock. 7:00 a.m. Dimly, in the back of her mind, she remembered Simon waking her with gentle kisses shortly before dawn, murmuring that he had to go, but would see her at breakfast. Now she wished he were still there to share whatever was going on.

"All right. I'll get some clothes on and be right there." She hung up and headed for the bathroom, where she stood under a cold shower just long enough to banish the lingering remnants of languor and ready herself, as best she could, for whatever lay ahead.

Dressed in crisp linen slacks and a pullover, with her hair falling around her shoulders and her skin bare of makeup, she took the stairs to Winston's office two at a time. He was there waiting, with a grim-faced Arthur Rutherford beside him.

Startled by the movie mogul's presence, Allegra looked questioningly from one man to the other. Winston ushered her into a chair and handed over a cup of coffee as he said, "Mr. Rutherford got a nasty surprise with his early morning tea. Namely, an anonymous letter warning that unless the maiden voyage is curtailed immediately, the *Silver Zephyr* will be sabotaged in flight."

"It fell out of the copy of the *International Herald Tribune* I had requested," the short, solidly built man explained quietly. "Not the usual sort of insert I'd expect."

"May I see it?" Allegra asked, holding out her hand.

Winston fetched the incriminating document from his desk and offered it to her. When she hesitated, he said, "Don't worry about fingerprints. This looks like a rather professional job, which means there are unlikely to be any. But even if there were, we have no way of detecting them."

"The police—" she began, only to be cut off as Rutherford shook his head.

"I've spoken with Tristan about this by phone, and we've agreed to keep the lid on it at least for the moment."

"You know, I presume, that this is not the first warning?" If she were breaching security by telling him that, too bad. She simply wasn't willing to withhold that sort of information under the present circumstances.

"Yes, Tristan told me when we spoke half an hour ago. I can't say I'm pleased not to have been informed sooner, but I can understand his reasoning. Just as I can understand the need to keep this latest development among ourselves. To do otherwise would be to invite panic."

"You don't think Mr. Levinson and Mr. Fletcher should be informed?" Winston asked, naming the other two major backers who were on board.

"Frankly, no. There's not a thing they could do to help, and we can't rule out the possibility that one or both of them may already know more about this than they should. So the less said about this to anyone, the better."

"Are you seriously suggesting one of the backers may be responsible for these threats?" Winston asked, making no effort to hide his skepticism.

"I'm suggesting we can't overlook any possibility,

however remote. Tristan continues to feel that these threats are meaningless. At this point I'm inclined to agree. I think our proper course right now is to increase our vigilance and take all sensible precautions without alarming anyone.''

Allegra couldn't help but notice that Rutherford was not offering that as a suggestion; it was a clear-cut order from a man who was obviously accustomed to being obeyed.

Taking the note from Winston, she studied it carefully. The stationery came from one of the desks in the *Silver Zephyr*'s library. Anyone on board could have picked it up.

The block letters were done in black fiberpoint strokes. The printing looked like something a particularly careful child might have done. There were no unique characteristics that leaped immediately to mind, nothing that might help to identify the person responsible for penning the warning and slipping it into Rutherford's newspaper.

''Why you?'' Allegra asked, glancing up at him. ''Do you have any idea why you were selected to receive this warning?''

''Perhaps I was simply the most accessible. Or perhaps whoever is responsible thought I'd be most likely to get nervous and insist on compliance. However, that is not the case. Everything to this point suggests we are engaged in a game of blindman's bluff. Until something happens to contradict that, I insist we sit tight.''

Allegra was about to respond, to point out that technically speaking something had already happened, when Winston prevented her. "All right, Mr. Rutherford," he said, ushering the man toward the door. "For the moment, at least, we are in agreement. I will alert my officers to be especially vigilant, but nothing will be done to cause any alarm among the passengers. Does that satisfy you?"

"Up to a point. I also want your word that if there are any further threats, I will be informed at once."

"Mr. Ward has already promised you that. Rest assured that his instructions, and yours, will be followed to the letter."

That seemed to satisfy the movie man, and he left a few moments later, presumably to finish his interrupted breakfast. When he was gone Winston turned back to Allegra and sighed deeply.

"What a pickle."

"Indeed. Are you sure Tristan is right to let this go on?"

"No, I'm not sure of anything right now, except that I will do my damndest to prevent the *Silver Zephyr* from coming to harm." His expression was stern and tenacious as he said, "I believe you know that I have the utmost respect for Tristan. Although he is still a relatively young man, he is both brilliant and daring. That is a rare combination which deserves encouragement."

"But . . . ?" At his quizzical look, she went on, "You've left something hanging, a qualification or condition of your trust in Tristan. What is it?"

"Only that this is my ship, as well as his. Without causing problems for the backers, I will do everything possible to protect her."

"You won't get any argument from me on that score. Is this a hypothetical discussion, or have you already done something?" Her dry tone made it clear which she suspected.

Winston grimaced. "Am I really that transparent?"

"No, but I flatter myself that I'm a better than average interpreter of human behavior. You aren't the sort to sit back and wait for a potential saboteur to take the next step. I'm willing to bet you've done something; I just don't know what."

"I've made a few inquiries," he admitted, propping himself up on a corner of the desk near her chair and refilling both their coffee cups. "Contacts of mine in New York and elsewhere have turned up some very interesting information. It seems that we have not one potential suspect, but a collection of them."

"Do go on," Allegra muttered. She had an idea of what might be coming and was already beginning to dread it. "I'm fascinated."

"Don't try to be witty this early in the morning. It's beyond you. Now, where was I? Oh, yes . . . suspects. That rock star I'm forced to dine with these days has had several brushes with the law, all concerning large amounts of cocaine. The tennis pro was involved in a shady currency transaction which brought him to the attention of the Treasury Department. Our couturier has apparently run on the wrong side of the import and labor regulations, enough to be threatened with severe fines."

"All very interesting, but hardly surprising. That doesn't make them saboteurs."

"No, but it does suggest a certain proclivity toward being blackmailed should the opportunity arise. At any rate, there is more of even greater interest." Having taken a sip of coffee, he continued. "Our financial genius, Mr. Levinson, is involved in even more deals than my contacts could determine, and believe me, that is impressive. Some of them are reputed to have gone rather disastrously wrong, to the extent that he is believed to have recently lost several million in cold, hard cash."

"If the reports I've heard about Bertrand Levinson are true, he could lose several tens of millions and not miss them."

"Perhaps, but no one can keep that up indefinitely, and if his luck has been bad for any length of time, he may be hurting. Which brings us to the next possibility, none other than our watchdog, Mr. Rutherford. He is something of a genuine mystery man. Everyone speaks of him with great awe, but no one seems to know much about him. In addition to his entertainment interest, he's worked with the Red Chinese, the Arabs, the South Africans and anyone else who could help him make a buck. He's considered tough as nails and extremely dangerous when angered."

"That ties in with everything I've heard about him, but it doesn't move him to the top of the suspect list. He has no reason to be angry about anything involving this venture."

"Perhaps not. Unfortunately, the same can't necessarily be said about your Mr. York."

Allegra took a hasty sip of coffee. It went down the

wrong way, and she coughed. Winston relieved her of
the cup and saucer, and patted her solicitously on the
back.

"Sorry to spring that on you, but I thought it best to
get it out in the open."

"Why . . ." she croaked, "did you ask your contacts to check up on Simon?"

"My dear girl, he *was* in the engine room during the
fire."

"When you didn't mention it at the time, I thought
you gave it no significance."

"Of course I did. His reason for being there was, to
say the least, flimsy. Although I have to admit his claim
to being a very close friend of Tristan's is true. You
know about their service together in Vietnam?"

"Yes."

"They've helped each other out numerous times
since. On the surface it appears to be an enviable
relationship. But a bit of wrinkle cropped up a few
years ago. It seems both Mr. Ward and Mr. York were
attracted to the same lady. She played them along for a
bit before deciding to accompany our Tristan on a
cruise of the Aegean, leaving your Simon to console
himself elsewhere. All the evidence suggests neither
one of them really cared; they went right on being the
best of friends. But I can't help but wonder . . ."

"Do you honestly think Simon has been carrying a
grudge against Tristan all these years just because of a
woman?" Allegra demanded incredulously.

"Never say 'just' in the context of an *affaire de
coeur*. Men have been known to go to incredibly
bizarre lengths when denied a lady's affections by a

rival. That's one area where civilization has yet to make much progress.''

''I don't believe you're serious. Simon is an intelligent, responsible man. He'd never get upset by something so petty.''

''What makes you think it was petty?''

What indeed? Her own experience with him was enough to tell her that he was an intensely passionate man capable of a level of emotion few could ever approach.

But she also believed him to be honorable, or she would never have trusted him enough to go to bed with him. She simply refused to accept the idea that he would spend years lulling a friend into a false sense of security so that he could seize an opportunity to destroy him.

For she had no doubt that Tristan's very spirit was woven into the *Silver Zephyr*. Were it to encounter tragedy, he would mourn as though for a lost child.

''If you insist on putting Simon on the suspect list, go right ahead. But don't expect me to agree.''

''There's no reason you have to, so long as that doesn't get in the way of your keeping track of him.''

''*What?*''

''You heard me. It's obvious that you and Mr. York are attracted to each other, so he's liable to be less suspicious of your company than of anyone else's. I just want you to keep your eyes open and report any curious behavior back to me.''

''You want me to spy on him!''

''Don't exaggerate. All I'm asking is that if you should, for example, find him one evening immersed in a manual on bomb construction, you'll let me know about it. All right?''

''And what will you be doing while I'm keeping tabs on Simon?''

Winston sighed and ran a weary hand through his hair. His expression was suddenly bleak as he said, ''I'll be doing the same with Ms. Ludlow. It seems she was implicated in an insurance fraud scheme about five years ago.''

''That's impossible. She would never have been hired if she had a record.''

''She doesn't. She was accused by one of the defendants, but there was never enough information to charge her. Under the circumstances, I'm afraid that means she has to be watched. Carefully.''

''That shouldn't be so difficult for you,'' Allegra suggested in a rather strained attempt at lightness.

He looked at her sadly. ''I'm afraid, my dear, the entire rest of this trip is going to be quite incredibly difficult.''

A short time later she remembered those words and admitted silently that they could not have been truer. Not even the glittering excitement of their arrival in London could still the doubts beginning to swirl through her mind.

As she joined Simon for breakfast she found herself wondering why he had left her so early. Was it merely out of a sense of discretion, or was something else involved?

Seeing him again even after such a brief separation brought home to her forcibly the impact he had on her.

Last night he had attuned her body to his so powerfully that she wondered if she would ever be able to stop wanting him. But even before then their spirits had begun to mingle as they found in each other shared traits of intelligence, humor and discipline.

Her response to him was so complete that, if she hadn't known better, she might have believed him a product of her own imagination. Certainly he was everything she had ever fantasized about finding in a man and even more, because he was real.

Or was he? What did she really know about him except what he had chosen to tell her and the gossip Winston had turned up?

Allegra sighed, impatient with herself. Simon caught the tiny sound and looked up, gazing at her over the breakfast menus.

"Something wrong?"

Since joining him at the window table, with its choice view of the mooring going on beneath them, she had hardly looked at him. Yet he dominated all her senses.

She was vividly aware of the tousled thickness of his hair glinting in the early sunlight, the burnished warmth of his skin stretched over perfectly molded bones that would make him compellingly attractive even when he was a very old man.

The cognac wool pullover he wore did nothing to disguise the powerful width of his shoulders. Her fingers tingled slightly as she remembered the velvety roughness of the hair covering his chest.

"Uh . . . no . . . nothing. I guess I'm just not quite awake yet."

He grinned provocatively. "I can't imagine why."

To her chagrin she felt her blush deepening. Determined to distract herself, she murmured, "I missed you this morning."

He broke a croissant in half and looked at her. "I missed you . . . even more than I'd expected. But if I'd stayed, we would never have made it out of your stateroom."

She could hardly argue with his reasoning, not when she was experiencing an insistent desire to return to the cool quiet of the big bed they had shared and forget all about the rest of the world.

A waiter arrived with the fresh orange juice and omelets they had ordered. The brief interruption gave her the chance to drag her unruly emotions under control. Barely in the nick of time, since she had been about to suggest that they forget all about everything else and just concentrate on each other.

That wouldn't do at all. Putting aside the doubts Winston's revelations had sparked, there was the simple fact that their relationship had already developed too precipitously. They barely knew each other, yet they had already shared the heights of physical pleasure.

Allegra shook her head thoughtfully. If anyone had told her even a few days ago that she would . . .

"Something wrong with your omelet?"

"What? Oh, no, it's fine. I was just . . . thinking. . . ."

Simon put down his fork and regarded her steadily. "I don't have to ask what about. You've been jumpier than a frog on a hot rock ever since you sat down."

"Where did you get that expression from?"

"Expression? Oh, everybody talks like that back where I grew up."

"Where was that?"

"Tennessee. But that's not what we were talking about. I realize everything's happened very fast. . . ."

"This conversation is certainly proof of that. I had no idea you came from Tennessee."

He took a long swallow of his orange juice before asking, "Where did you think I came from?"

"California, I guess, since you'd mentioned working there."

"I ended up there after 'Nam. How about you? New York girl?"

"Brooklyn." She grinned at his questioning look. "There is a difference, you know. We used to be a separate city, and in some ways still are."

"But you crossed the river to the Big Apple with considerable success."

"Not according to my family." Her candor surprised her. She hadn't meant to say that, to reveal so much of herself.

Simon reached out a hand, taking hold of hers and turning it over, gently rubbing the palm with his thumb. "Want to tell me about it?"

She laughed a bit shakily. "I'm not sure I have much choice. You seem to bring out a certain reckless lack of reserve in me."

"Why should that worry you? I'm not going to take advantage of any confidences we share."

Her silent scrutiny of him was enough to express her doubts. Releasing her hand, Simon sat back in his chair. "Something's happened to you since last night. You're having second thoughts . . . regrets . . . whatever. I was afraid of this."

"Why?"

"Because even though it was predictable, I didn't know how to prevent it. I should have waited before taking you to bed, but I couldn't. You're just too much for me." The words might have been offered humorously, but they were not. He was completely serious, or at least he was being very careful to give that impression.

Slowly she said, "Simon, I honestly don't regret what happened last night. It was far too beautiful . . . and too important to me. But we're bound to have doubts about each other until we share more of ourselves. As incredible as it may sound, we're still strangers in certain ways."

"There's an easy solution to that," he told her cheerfully. "We need to spend more time together."

Despite herself, she laughed. Suddenly the day didn't seem quite so gloomy as it had earlier. Whatever was or was not going on between her and Simon, whatever danger did or did not stalk the *Silver Zephyr*, the sky outside their window was still a radiantly cloudless blue, and the ancient city of London beckoned with the same magic it had used to seduce visitors for centuries.

"Do you know," she mused, "the only times I've been here have been business trips. I've seen hardly anything except the insides of hotels and restaurants." She glanced at him hopefully to see if he had taken the hint.

To her delight Simon looked properly horrified. Pushing back his chair, he said, "Then let's remedy that right away. I promise, by nightfall you'll feel like a genuine tourist."

She did. Well before the long spring twilight settled over the city her feet ached and her head whirled with a kaleidoscope of impressions and images. She and Simon had "done" the town from Piccadilly Circus and Marble Arch to Buckingham Palace, Westminster Abbey, Parliament and the Tower.

They laughed at the antics of the sea lions in the zoo, brought flowers from an old lady in Mayfair and browsed for bargains at the Portobello Road market.

The day took on the aura of an enchanted interlude. Allegra had never taken a vacation before, and was therefore unfamiliar with the special feelings that came from being in a place, yet not part of it. Free to enjoy all the best it offered without confronting the problems or responsibilities.

It was a heady experience, one she promised to give herself again. No sooner was the silent vow made than she realized that anywhere she might go would seem stale and arid without Simon's presence.

Whatever attractions London might hold on its own were magnified a thousand times by sharing them with him. They pointed out particularly interesting or amusing vignettes to each other, often with no more than a smile and a glance. They compared what they were seeing to other places they had been, in the process talking about their lives without strain or artifice.

Allegra thought she had traveled widely, but Simon outdid her. He had been almost everywhere except—as he pointed out—both poles. "The closest I've gotten was Tierra del Fuego, down at the tip of South America, and that was cold enough. I felt no urge to go on."

"What took you there?"

"The creakiest, most disreputable freighter ever to plow the seas. When I left home, at sixteen, I lied about my age and signed on with the Merchant Marines. Did two years with them before joining the Army. Between one and the other, I got around pretty well."

"What made you go out on your own so early?"

"I think I knew it was then or never. You see, I'm one of those rare individuals who admits to coming from a genuinely terrific, happy family. No one could ask for better parents than mine. They were married for forty years before Dad died. Mom's managed to hold up pretty well since then, mainly because of my brothers and sisters, who are among the best people I know. If I'd stayed any longer I would have been too damn comfortable, and I'd never have wanted to leave."

"Have you ever regretted it?"

"Sometimes. I'm an uncle half-a-dozen times over, but I'd like to have children of my own. I've moved around so much that I've almost forgotten what it feels like to have a real home, but whenever I go back on a visit I'm reminded, and I envy what I see."

He was silent for a moment, his gaze turned inward at memories she could not yet fathom. Then he shook them off and smiled down at her. "This morning you started to tell me about your family, but we got sidetracked. Why don't they approve of what you've achieved?''

''It's not that they don't approve . . . exactly. They just don't understand why I wanted it so much, instead of the things they thought I should care about.''

''Like a husband and children?''

''Yes. Oh, don't get me wrong; my folks aren't throwbacks to another era or anything like that. It's just that they've always put family first, and to them that means making an active effort to find the right spouse and then settling down to build a life together. When they realized how little appeal that had for me, they were bewildered.''

''I don't see why,'' he said, genuinely puzzled. ''You had to find yourself before you could think of finding someone else.''

That was *exactly* how Allegra had always felt, and the shock of hearing her most private thoughts expressed by someone else held her very still. Simon saw her surprise and smiled gently.

''There's nothing strange about your feelings. It seems to me that both our families started out with very little and worked their way up to a lot more. In the process they had no chance to think of anything except survival. But they gave their children the opportunity to go beyond that, without even realizing how precious that gift is.''

''Maybe I should bring you home with me and have you explain it to them.'' The words were out before she had a chance to consider their implication. Biting her lip, she glanced up at him warily.

Far from appearing put off, Simon looked pleased

and even . . . relieved? Was it possible she was not alone in her sense of vulnerability? He seemed to be every bit as uncertain and concerned as she was, and just as anxious to make their relationship work.

For the first time since the ecstatic hours they had shared, she let herself believe that there might really be a future for them. A tremor of pleasure coursed through her. Even as she cautioned herself not to hope for too much, she couldn't help but contemplate the enticing potential of a future with Simon.

To have the right to lie beside him every night, to know the joy of being in his arms without fear of what the morning would bring, to stand beside him and share both his triumphs and his failures, was so dizzyingly a prospect that she could barely grasp it.

Never before had she even seriously considered making a commitment of that nature to a man, yet now she found she could think of little else. Wryly, she had to admit that there seemed to be a hidden part of herself capable of making decisions and taking actions without consulting with the more rational side that liked to think it ran everything.

That sensible part of her was chattering away even now, insisting she go slowly and not hope for too much. But the rush of happiness surging through her made that voice very dim. She could barely hear it any longer, and didn't miss it a bit.

Chapter 9

No matter how many times she visited Paris, or how accustomed she became to its elegant beauty, it always held a special fascination for Allegra. She could well understand why poets and artists had immortalized it through the ages, and why so many still considered it to be the center of a very special way of life.

For all the changes recent decades had wrought—the congested highways ringing the city, and the office towers challenging the Belle Epoque skyline—nothing could undermine the essential magic of the place.

Especially not when it was seen from above at night while standing safe and warm in Simon's arms. She nestled closer to him, relishing the hardness of his chest pressing against her cheek. A soft chuckle rumbled deep with him as his embrace tightened.

"Who says the Eiffel Tower is hokey?" he murmured.

"Cynics."

He tangled his hands in the silken skeins of her hair and tipped her head back gently. "People who don't know what this feels like."

"What's 'this'?"

"The two of us, here, now, concentrating on each other."

"Mmmm . . . I think I like you in concentrated doses. Does wonders for my ego."

An eyebrow arched above one remarkably gentle, indulgent gray eye. "Why's that?"

"Didn't you notice in that restaurant tonight? You were easily the most attractive man, and every woman there knew it."

"Were there other women there?"

"Nice . . . all the right answers."

"All I know is that I thought I was going to have to fight at least a couple of guys off to keep you to myself."

"Don't be silly. They don't allow fighting in the Tour d'Argent."

"That was some fancy place, ma'am," he said in his best Tennessee drawl. "Best meat loaf I've ever had."

Her laughter was muffled against the black velvet of his dinner jacket. "I'm glad you liked the pâté. What did you think of the boullabaisse?"

"You mean that fish stew? It wasn't bad. Good apple pie, too."

"The *tarte aux pommes* is a house specialty."

"I've got one or two of those myself. Care to get acquainted with them?"

Her hazel eyes opened wider, dark pools of swirling gold and moss secrets. "You mean I haven't already?"

"Honey, last night was just the appetizer. And I don't mind telling you, I am about ready for the main course."

Allegra had a sudden vision of herself laid out naked and nicely sauced for his delectation. The picture had a certain appeal. But some perverse feminine instinct drove her to play the game out for all it was worth.

"Didn't you say we were going to drop by a casino?"

"Actually, I'm not much of a betting man."

She ignored the hint and went on blithely. "I've never been to one, but I've always thought it would be fun."

"I'll make a deal with you; we'll go, but we won't stay long. How's that?"

"Well . . . if you really want to make it an early night."

"*Allegra* . . ." The warning note told her that his tolerance for her teasing was wearing thin. Laughing softly, she let him take her hand and lead her past a group of amused tourists to the elevator that carried them swiftly back to ground level.

The cab he had hired for the evening was waiting. The driver shot them a benignly tolerant look as they settled themselves into the back seat, with Allegra's head resting on Simon's broad shoulder.

"Where to now, monsieur?"

"La Bonne Chance. The lady wants to try her luck."

"They stay open until dawn."

"Wait for us. We won't be longer than an hour."

The driver flashed him a quick grin of male understanding. "As you say, monsieur."

"Where did you learn to speak French?" Allegra asked as the cab pulled away.

Distracted by the petal-smooth texture of her cheek, he answered automatically. "Here and there."

She drew back slightly. "Where?"

Her patient persistence amused him. Laughing, he hugged her closer and rested his chin on the top of her head. "I picked it up in bits and pieces, starting when I was with the Merchant Marines and later in Indochina. The grammar, syntax, all the rest of it came in college. It's been . . . useful."

"Do you speak any other languages?"

"I can get by in Spanish, and I won't starve if I'm set down someplace where they only speak Italian. What about you?"

"A smattering of this and that. Whatever I've needed in business." She chuckled as a memory flashed through her mind. "I saw a phrase book once that gave all the correct things to say while making love in seven languages."

"Seven? At the same time? That's a bit crowded, isn't it?"

"Silly. You know what I mean."

"Did you buy the book?"

"No . . . I didn't expect to ever have any need of it."

"You don't," he whispered audaciously in her ear. "The sweet little cries you make would be understood in any language."

Allegra turned bright red. She felt the sudden burning rush of blood to her cheeks and was certain she had lit up like a beacon. It would serve him right if she blinded him with the intensity.

What business did he have reminding her so graphically of what had passed between them in the secret hours of the night? Turning her insides to liquid heat and her legs to jelly? Making her regret that she had ever suggested they go to the casino and wish instead that they were on their way back to her stateroom?

When she tried to pull away from him, his grip tightened inexorably. Humor, mixed with apology, softened his voice. "I'm sorry, honey, but I couldn't resist. You're just too much fun to tease . . . among other things."

She was saved from the necessity of answering by the taxi driver announcing their arrival at the club. "I will park across the street, monsieur."

"We'll find you. As I said, in about an hour."

La Bonne Chance was among the most luxurious and exclusive casinos in Europe. Operating as a private club, it was free to offer the ultimate in entertainment and services to a discerning clientele.

Not surprisingly, quite a few of the *Silver Zephyr*'s passengers were on hand, drawn by the high-stakes betting and the *laissez-faire* attitude of a management which was known to turn a blind eye to assignations of all types.

The glittering Louis Quinze interior, with its ornate

ceiling murals, crystal chandeliers and brocade walls, was well matched by the lavishly dressed men and women flitting among the baccarat and roulette tables.

"Do you know the rules of either of those games?" Simon asked as he took her arm and led her toward the center of the main room.

"No," she informed him cheerfully, "but I'm a fast learner."

"Yes," he drawled, "I know. But do me a favor and stick close to me."

That was hardly a great concession. Just as at the restaurant, Simon was coming in for more than his fair share of feminine attention. But now, whether because of the setting or the late hour, there was a faintly predatory gleam in the eyes of the women who watched him that set Allegra's nerves on edge.

She was so preoccupied that she didn't notice what was patently obvious to Simon, namely that her tall, ripely curved form, encased in a burgundy velvet dress that left her alabaster shoulders and arms bare and clung to her high breasts and narrow waist, was making her the focal point of male interest.

His hand tightened, drawing her closer against the steely length of his body. If just one of those bastards thought he was going to make it to first base with her, he had another thought coming.

"Simon, you're hurting me."

Her slightly husky voice reached him through a red haze of burgeoning outrage. He came back to himself with a jolt. "Honey, I'm sorry. . . ." His voice shook slightly. He couldn't bear the thought of hurting her. It was a shock to realize how much more readily he would endure pain himself rather than allow her to suffer in even the smallest way.

"Hey," she said lightly, "it's okay. I'm not exactly breakable, you know."

No, she wasn't. She was a strong, resilient, determined woman. The kind a man could depend on for the long haul. When she loved, she would do so fiercely. And she would never let her man down.

Why was he thinking about what it would be like to be loved by her? In his present state that was an added torment he most certainly did not need.

Finding two empty seats side by side at one of the baccarat tables, he resolutely turned his attention to the game. "It looks deceptively simple," he explained. "The idea is to collect cards with a point total as close to twenty-one as possible, without going over it. A kid could play it, only in a casino like this it's very much an adult's game."

"Because of the amount of money involved?" She had seen the stack of chips on the table and done a rough computation that stunned her. By even a conservative estimate, thousands of dollars were changing hands at an incredible rate, mostly in the direction of the house.

"I see you get the idea," Simon murmured. "Now you know why I don't want you going off on your own."

"All right, just don't blame me if I turn out to be bad luck."

But in fact she seemed to be exactly the opposite. Simon had been playing for some fifteen minutes, and winning steadily, when a new arrival slid into the seat opposite them.

Bertrand Levinson nodded courteously. "Nice to see you both. You seem to be on a streak, Mr. York. I hope you don't mind if I see what I can do to break it?"

The courtly, white-haired gentleman hardly looked like a formidable opponent, but something in his pale blue eyes must have warned Simon, for he began to play with judicious restraint. Far from being handicapped by such caution, he was rewarded by even more dramatic wins that quickly stripped Levinson of what Allegra, at least, regarded as a very significant amount of money.

When some ten thousand dollars in chips lay on the table, with Simon having already won a similar amount, Levinson looked up with apparent unconcern. Quietly he said, "I'd like to raise the stakes."

Simon's hands were steady against the green felt cloth. "To what?"

"From one thousand a chip to five."

"You seem to take this a great deal more seriously than I do."

"All things are relative. I don't bet more than I can afford to lose."

"In that case," Simon said dryly, "I won't feel guilty when I win."

Coming from another man, such confidence might have seemed graceless. But Simon had done no more than state what turned out to be inevitable. Within another quarter of an hour he had won fifty thousand dollars, and the crowd that had gathered around the table was in ecstasies.

Bertrand Levinson, however, was not so pleased.

For all his contention that he could afford to be beaten, he clearly did not relish the experience. His smoothly shaved face with its aristocratic features was slightly mottled, and his mouth trembled as he raised a hand, summoning one of the casino managers to his side.

"I'd like to raise my limit for this evening."

The man glanced up toward what looked like a mirrored wall at one end of the room. He hesitated a moment, then nodded. "Of course, Monsieur Levinson. Will an additional quarter of a million be sufficient?"

Despite his rapidly souring mood, the financier managed a tight smile. "I certainly hope so. Unless, of course, Mr. York's luck refuses to turn."

"You'll have to count me out," Simon said as he rose and scooped the chips into his hand. When Levinson started to protest, he added, "I promised Ms. Whitney we'd only stay an hour."

That wasn't precisely true, but she had no intention of quibbling. The sooner they got out of there, the happier she would be. What had started out as no more than a mild amusement was rapidly turning into something a good deal graver.

The flat determination in Simon's eyes must have convinced the financier that his mind could not be changed. He shrugged philosophically. "Another time." Moments later, as they were walking toward the cashier's cage, he was deeply immersed in a contest with another player.

"How can he lose like that and go right on gambling?" Allegra asked as they waited for the chips to be converted into a check. ''I know he's supposed to be fabulously wealthy, but if he does this very often, even he'll run out of money eventually.''

''That doesn't seem to worry him.''

''It has to. Some of his business ventures have gone very poorly lately. With his luck that bad, he shouldn't be gambling at all.''

''How did you know about that?'' Simon asked as they left the casino and got back into the cab. He sounded only mildly curious, but Allegra wasn't fooled. She could feel the tension radiating from him.

It had begun as soon as they walked into the casino and increased steadily the whole time he was playing against Levinson. She suspected it had nothing whatsoever to do with any concern Simon might have felt about his own luck. But neither did it have the sensual quality of the tautness she had sensed in him earlier. For a man who had just won fifty thousand dollars, he seemed singularly uneasy.

''What do you plan to do with the money?'' she asked in an effort to distract him.

''Money? Oh, that. I don't know. Invest it, probably.''

''Do you have a lot of investments?''

''No, just a few that particularly interest me. I'm certainly nowhere near Levinson's league, but then, almost no one is.''

''It's his behavior that's bothering you, isn't it?''

He glanced down at her and nodded ruefully. ''There's a recklessness about him that worries me. He tries to hide it, to appear as though he's only gambling

for amusement, but I sensed something more. Almost
. . . desperation.''

"I know what you mean. It bothered me, too. Do
you think it's possible that he's a compulsive gam-
bler?''

"A couple of hours ago I would have said no. It
doesn't seem likely that anyone with that problem
could reach the heights Levinson has attained. But now
I have to wonder. Maybe he's managed to strike some
sort of compromise in his life where he keeps his
gambling separate from everything else.''

"Or maybe everything he does is gambling and he's
just had unusually good luck up until now.''

"I'd hate to think that's true. After all, he's an
important part of this venture.''

"Do you know exactly how important?'' Allegra
asked.

"No, but I intend to find out.'' After helping her out
of the cab, he paid the driver. Together they strolled
toward the boarding ramp, past the officers on security
duty who, recognizing them, waved them by.

Their playfully flirtatious mood of earlier in the
evening had not returned by the time Simon escorted
her to her stateroom door. He stood for a moment,
trailing a finger along the soft curve of her jaw, before
he smiled wryly.

"Against all my inclinations, I must ask you to
excuse me for a few minutes. I want to check in with
Tristan and find out exactly what he knows about
Levinson.''

Allegra was disappointed, but not surprised. Nor

was she disposed to pretend that he had no reason to return to her. Events of the previous night had forged an understanding between them that, while by no means complete, did not allow for such deception.

"All right. I have some papers I need to go over anyway. But," she added lightly, "I will expect a full report."

He dropped a gentle kiss on her mouth. "I won't be long."

She hoped not. While it was true there was work that required her attention, she doubted she would be able to concentrate on it. Not while she was waiting for Simon to return and make love to her again.

She shook her head mockingly. What a position to find herself in. Cool, self-contained Allegra Whitney, who had smilingly turned her back on more men than she could remember, caught by a mysterious adventurer whose motives were still dubious, but whose attractions were irresistible.

Slipping out of her gown and removing the rest of her clothes, she tried to pin down her continued inability to simply accept Simon as a concerned friend of Tristan's who was standing in for him on the trip. Why didn't she believe that? Was she still seeking reasons to distrust him despite all that had passed between them? Or were her most deeply rooted instincts trying to tell her something?

Through the fog of sensual anticipation it was difficult to turn her mind to other thoughts, but she did so determinedly. Stepping under the shower, she began to construct a mental list of all the attributes she had seen in him that pointed to something more than an amateur's interest.

The sponge stopped in midair, dripping soap as she stared at the marble wall without seeing it. The quality she sensed in Simon was professionalism. Whenever the subject of the *Silver Zephyr*'s safety came up he projected an aura of capability and confidence that suggested this was not the first time he had faced such a problem.

Was that simply a holdover from his experiences in Vietnam, which must have accustomed him to danger, or was something more involved? And if she were right, if he was more than simply the engineer he claimed to be, were his skills truly being used to protect the airship, or to harm her?

She toweled herself dry and slipped into an ivory lace peignoir, all the while telling herself that she had already made up her mind in favor of Simon's honesty and integrity, otherwise she would never have embarked on such an intimate relationship with him. This was no time to be having second thoughts.

Especially not since he was knocking at the door. Hurrying to admit him, she found him with his tie undone and his dinner jacket hanging open, a bottle of champagne and two glasses in his hands.

"You the lady who ordered room service?"

Falling in with the game, she nodded. "You look like exactly what I had in mind. Come on in."

"You single women sure are pushy." Ambling past her, he turned to wrap a steely arm around her waist and pull her to him. "Good thing pushy turns me on."

"I'm beginning to think everything turns you on," Allegra laughed, freeing herself and setting the glasses on the table as he began uncorking the champagne. "What did Tristan have to say?"

"Not much. He still thinks Levinson is on the up-and-up, but he's going to check it out."

"How's he feeling?"

"Like a bear with a sore head. I get the impression he's not the world's best patient."

"I'll bet! He's too strong and vigorous to put up with any disability, even a temporary one."

"I suppose you know you look ravishing?" Simon said as he handed her one of the fluted glasses.

She took a sip and batted her eyelashes. "Too bad. I was aiming for ravishable."

He laughed boldly. "I wish you weren't so coy. You never give me any idea where I stand with you."

"Are we going to stand?" she inquired with a pout.

He took the glass from her and carried it, along with his own, over to the bedside table, then proceeded to strip off the blue satin coverlet and remove his jacket. "Not," he informed her succinctly, "if I have anything to say about it."

Through the thick fringe of her lashes, Allegra watched him remove his shoes and unbutton his shirt. She didn't know why she should suddenly feel abashed about looking at him, but it seemed to have something to do with his matter-of-fact approach to going to bed with her.

It was as though she had no more barriers or secrets left, and he could treat her with the relaxed amicability appropriate to a wife of a dozen years. That was jumping just a bit too far ahead, and was rather more than she could handle at the moment.

Where were the seduction, the romance, the giddy sense of discovery and elation she had known the night before? Making no claims to being very sexually liberated, she wanted all that again, and more.

But Simon didn't seem predisposed to give it. At least not until he had removed his shirt, taken another swallow of champagne and turned back to her with a grin that could only be described as . . . roguish?

"You're quite right, you know," he said as he strolled toward her. *"Ravishable* is definitely the right word."

Something about his deceptively lazy approach made her wary. She took a step back, but not quickly enough to evade his sudden lunge. Having been scooped up into his arms, she was cárried across the room and lowered very firmly onto the bed.

His sudden aggression prompted a nervous laugh. She twisted slightly in his hands, trying to get free, only to discover she could not. The teasing had disappeared from his face, replaced by a taut anticipation that sent tremors through her.

Trapping her gently with his body, he lowered his mouth to hers. "You taste sweet," he murmured as he nibbled at her lips. "Just like I remember from last night. All day I've been thinking that had to be a dream . . . I've never found anything so perfect . . . only you . . . and me . . . together."

Allegra's hands were clutching at his bare back, her

senses whirling as she yielded again to the overwhelming mastery of his touch. Lean fingers, their tips roughened by calluses, brushed the lace away from her shoulders. His lips were warm and searching, nuzzling at the soft curves of her breasts until he had bared them fully to him.

As he drew a straining nipple within his mouth, suckling her tenderly, she cried out. Her hands fastened convulsively on his broad leather belt, seeking the buckle. She unfastened it and swiftly undid his trousers, reaching within them to knead his hard buttocks.

Simon laughed deep in his throat. "Temptress . . . you're supposed to be getting ravished, not the other way around."

"Why not?" she demanded pertly. "In fact, I've decided that sounds like a good idea." Moving too swiftly for him to react, she sat up suddenly and pushed him onto his back.

Without bothering to cover her breasts, she bent over him, tugging his trousers off and dropping them onto the floor along with the rest of his clothes. Simon stared at her bemusedly. Her hair tumbled around her bare shoulders; her eyes glowed with provocative fires; her lips were full and ripe, slightly swollen from his impassioned kisses.

At that instant he recognized her for all that she was, the epitome of everything he had sought in a woman: spirited, beautiful, intelligent. A woman as comfortable with her own femininity as she was with his masculinity. The perfect complement to himself, and all he had ever dreamed for his future.

That realization made him tremble as much as the touch of her mouth and hands as she moved over him. Tentatively at first, then with growing confidence, she explored him as thoroughly as he had her.

The responses of his big, hard body fascinated her. His flat nipples surrounded by crisp curls of chestnut hair were as sensitive as her own. They tightened perceptibly as she brushed her tongue over them before tasting the burnished warmth of his skin.

Simon groaned deep in his throat. He sensed her need to be certain she could touch him like this, but he had to doubt how much more he would be able to bear.

When she stepped away for a moment, smiling down at him with provocative tenderness, he took a long, shuddering breath. The peignoir slipped from her, landing in a lacy heap around her slender ankles. She stepped out of it gracefully and unconsciously tossed her head back, letting her hair fall in thick, gleaming waves down her back.

The hand he held out to her shook slightly. "Come back here."

She made no pretense at refusal. Obediently lying down beside him, she set her hands to wandering over him until at last his great control was broken. The sound of her name on his lips was an almost feral growl as he moved abruptly, seizing both her wrists and tumbling her onto her back even as his sinewy thigh urged hers apart.

"Enough," he groaned thickly. "I feel as though I'm about to burst."

She moved against him erotically. "Go right ahead

. . . but inside me, please.'' This last was little more than a breathless moan as she arched her hips, offering him the haven of her body.

Simon waited no longer. His heart was hammering against the cage of his ribs, and his breath came in tortured gasps as he drove into her. Never in his life had he wanted anything so badly as he wanted to find his completion within this woman. Not even during the grotesque days and nights in Vietnam, when death had been a constant presence at his shoulder, had the life force driven him so remorselessly.

Yet despite the raging firestorm of his own need, he never lost awareness of her response. Not until he felt the long, velvety contractions of fulfillment undulate deep within her did he yield, making of his body and his spirit a gift of love.

Chapter 10

WAKING IN SIMON'S ARMS WAS A BLISSFUL INTRODUC-
tion to what promised to be a delightful day.

They had awakened twice in the middle of the night
to make love again, stopping only when exhaustion
finally claimed them both. Even then they didn't move
apart, but slept entwined in each other's arms.

The first sound she heard when consciousness finally
returned was the slow, rhythmic beat of his heart
beneath her ear. Without opening her eyes, she smiled
and stirred against him.

The warm, slightly musky scent of his skin filled her
nose. Crisp hairs tickled her chin. She was cocooned in
male strength and gentleness, held a willing prisoner
beside the virile body that had so enraptured hers.

She snuggled closer, slipping her smooth leg between his. He stirred slightly and a big hand rose to cup

the back of her head. Turning over, he drew her under him and found her mouth with unerring accuracy.

Their lovemaking was slow and gentle, silent except for the soft cries that escaped them both at the end. When it was over Allegra felt not pleasantly tired, as she would have expected, but vitally, thrillingly alive. Simon shared the feeling.

He propped himself above her and grinned rakishly. "Good morning."

"You sure beat an alarm clock."

"That's my special wake-up service. Like it?"

"No, I just went along to be polite." A muted giggle escaped her.

He bit the tip of her chin. "I guess I'll just have to try harder."

"If you do, I'll die. I just barely survived that."

He lay back, his arms folded behind his head, and scratched his chest lazily. "Me, too. But it's a hell of a way to go."

She was silent for a moment before she collected herself enough to ask, "Mind if I use the shower first?"

"Go ahead. I'll order breakfast." He hesitated a moment, looking at her uncertainly. "Do you mind if I have mine brought here?"

His concern for her feelings sent a little burst of pleasure through her. It was reassuring to know that the same man who could raise her to such heights of ecstasy could also be sensitive to more mundane matters.

"I'd mind if you didn't," she said lightly.

She was standing in the shower, her face tilted up to

the spray, when he joined her. Half hoping he would, she had listened alertly for any sign of his approach. When the door creaked slightly, she smiled.

He stepped in behind her and grasped her waist gently, nuzzling her neck as she teased, "Hey, this is supposed to be a private room."

"You should have read the fine print in the brochure. Every private room comes with a back scrubber."

"Oh . . . well, as long as you intend to make yourself useful, I guess it's okay."

"Mmmm, better than that." He pressed closer, letting her buttocks rub against his flat abdomen. Sliding his hands up, he cupped her breasts gently. A soft chuckle escaped him as he found her taut nipples. "You, madam, are insatiable."

"Me?" She moved experimentally against him. "What's that I'm feeling?"

"Just a healthy male, ma'am, in his prime and glad of it."

"That," she informed him as she turned around, "makes two of us."

Simon gazed down at her with cheerful lechery. "By the way, I do front scrubbing, too."

"Never let it be said I stood between a man and his work."

He was quite good at it, she thought long moments later. Front and back, she glowed with his touch. Long, enthralling minutes passed before she could endure no more. With her legs threatening to give out from under her, it only seemed fair to return the favor.

The mirrors had long since misted over, and water was collecting around their feet before they recovered themselves enough to leave the shower. Allegra stood docilely before him as Simon wrapped her in a bath sheet, drying her as carefully as though she were a child.

Standing so close to him, she was struck all over again by the differences between them. When they were dressed and out together in public the conventions of civilization hid much. But as they were now, alone and still touched by the glow of their lovemaking, her perceptions were altered.

She saw not simply the witty, urbane man whose company she enjoyed so much, but a powerful, resolute male more than capable of claiming what he wanted and keeping it close. A shiver ran through her as she realized how susceptible she was to his strength.

All her adult life she had been alone, and even before then, as a child, she had learned to rely on herself. Not because her family and friends were weak, but because they wanted different things and dreamed different dreams.

Now, at last, she had found a man who was truly the other, hitherto missing, part of herself. A man she was not afraid to trust, who seemed able to understand and accept both her strengths and weaknesses. A man she could build a future with, and grow old beside.

Or was she fooling herself? She shied away from the thought, knowing that to confront it head-on would be to fall off a precipice onto the jagged rocks of disappointment and disillusionment. Yet she had to at least peer over the edge.

She had known him only a few days under circumstances conducive to fantasizing. She had hurtled into a relationship that under ordinary circumstances would have taken months to develop. And now she was reaping the inevitable consequences, not knowing where she stood with him or what was likely to happen between them when the voyage ended and they went their separate ways, she back to work in New York and he home to California.

Shipboard romance. The phrase stung. She had always viewed such relationships with derision, if not absolute contempt, feeling pity for people who could indulge in such casual couplings. Yet wasn't she doing the same?

The shiver turned to a tremor of mingled fear and denial. She swayed against Simon, seeking the warm, hard reassurance of his body. His arms went around her instantly, offering comfort she gladly accepted.

"Honey," he asked with soft concern, "are you all right?"

She smiled into his chest, feeling the thick hair tickle her cheek. "Yes, or I will be, if you ever break down and feed me."

He laughed, relieved. But his eyes were still watchful as he let go of her long enough to pull on a robe, then scooped her into his arms and, despite her half-hearted protests, carried her back to the bed.

"Now what kind of gentleman would I be if I let a lady starve? You just stay right there and I'll find out what's keeping breakfast."

In point of fact, nothing was. The discreet steward had left a covered tray outside their door. Retrieving it, Simon grinned at her. "This will get your strength back up in no time."

Propped up on her elbows, she watched as he spread out a veritable feast of eggs Benedict, fresh orange juice, coffee, croissants, jams and fruit. Her stomach growled indelicately.

When she flushed, he laughed and leered teasingly. "I like a woman with a good appetite."

"I thought we'd already established that," she muttered dryly, reaching for a croissant. It was sweet and flaky in her mouth, so good that she was prompted to have another.

"Eat your eggs," Simon instructed. "You need the protein." Before she could respond one way or the other, he cut a forkful and maneuvered it toward her mouth.

Swallowing, she found she wanted another bite and dug in with a will. In silence punctuated by long glances and tender laughter, they finally managed to finish breakfast. Simon went off to his stateroom to dress as Allegra readied herself to face the day.

Dressed in a bright blue skirt and daffodil-yellow top, she slipped her bare feet into sandals and swept her hair back from her lightly tanned face. As she took the long way up to Winston's office she paused to unobtrusively check on the overall condition of the public rooms—excellent—and the mood of the passengers—relaxed, yet with a fine edge of excitement that meant the trip was giving them everything it had promised.

The several hundred strangers who had tromped up the boarding ramp a few days before were now a congenial community of, if not friends, at least acquaintances. On so large a vessel each individual was free to strike up relationships or refrain, according to personal inclination.

The sense of being part of something special created a certain benign smugness nicely leavened by the great cities they were visiting. They were in a separate world, all right, but one whose boundaries merged at certain select points with those of other equally glamorous and exciting realities.

And that, Allegra reflected, was the essential attraction of the *Silver Zephyr*, something she had dimly understood in the back of her mind but had not been able to crystalize before this voyage.

It was a dream of how life could be, made solid and believable by its proximity to the rest of the world. Cruise ships, which made port in artificial environments created to cater strictly to tourists, could not rival it. Neither could the jets that diminished great distances to the level of banalities. Only the *Silver Zephyr* could combine fantasy and reality to such a stunning degree. For that reason alone, it deserved to be protected.

Winston thought so, too. He was finishing a second cup of tea when she arrived in his office, and motioned her to a chair with a slight frown. "I've got some rather bad news, I'm afraid. To begin with, Tristan is back in the hospital."

"Back? I hadn't realized he'd been discharged."

"He wasn't. The young fool checked out despite his doctor's warning that he had a concussion and needed to be kept under observation. Apparently he had some idea of flying over here to join us. His cleaning lady found him unconscious on the floor in his apartment and called an ambulance. The word is that he'll be all right, but he's strictly out of touch for the next few days.''

Allegra inhaled raggedly. She knew Tristan tended to give far more attention to the well-being of his various inventions than to his own, but this was going a bit far. He had seriously endangered himself. Not for the first time, she thought he needed a keeper and said as much.

''He walks around in a fog most of the time, dreaming up some new creation. Somebody needs to bring him down to earth, at least enough to look after him.''

Winston cast her a rueful glance. ''For a while, I thought you might be the one to do that. After all, the two of you get along very well.''

''Because we're friends. But it's going to take more than that to make Tristan look after himself. I just hope they have him tied down to that hospital bed with good, strong ropes.''

''Indeed. Pending his recovery, we have another problem to deal with.''

Suspecting she was going to regret knowing, Allegra asked, ''What's that?''

''My contacts in New York have turned up some additional information on Mr. York. Apparently you were quite correct to think his name sounded familiar. He was in the news a few months back.''

Consulting a note pad on his desk, Winston said, ''Mr. York founded a small computer company located in California. The firm attracted considerable interest because he was said to be working on a revolutionary new microchip that would dramatically increase the power of small computers. Around the beginning of the year the company went public with a spectacular stock offering that turned Mr. York into an overnight millionaire. But immediately afterward trading was stopped when another company charged him with pirating their design for the chip.''

''He was accused of stealing someone else's work?''

''Exactly. Mr. York denied it, and no conclusive proof has been offered, but his reputation was damaged. By then, however, it was too late to have much effect on his fortunes. He had made, as the saying goes, a killing.''

''And the chip he was working on . . . ?''

''Has yet to appear on the market.''

A hollow sense of dread opened up in Allegra, growing wider with each breath. She was torn between instinctive faith in Simon and logical skepticism.

What, after all, did she really know about him beyond the fact that he was a considerate, amicable companion and tender, giving lover? That suggested facets of his character she was tempted to carry over into all aspects of his life, but perhaps that temptation should be resisted.

For the sake of her own self preservation, perhaps she needed to back up a pace and take a cold, hard look at the situation.

Suspecting that it might be a good idea to do so was one thing; actually doing it was quite another. Some deeply rooted part of herself, beyond the influence of reason, demanded that she trust Simon.

Winston took in her deepening pallor and shook his
head regretfully. He poured a fresh cup of tea and
gently pressed it into her hands. "I'm sorry, my dear. I
should have prepared you better."

"No . . . it's all right. I just need to get my thoughts
in order." She took a sip of the tea, then looked up at
him shakily. "You probably felt the same way when
you found out about Kirsten's implication in that
insurance fraud."

The dull flush that passed fleetingly over his smoothly shaven cheeks confirmed her guess. What might to
outsiders look like an improbable, if not impossible,
relationship was developing at a pace matching her
own involvement with Simon.

Granted Kirsten and Winston had known each other
a good deal longer, but it was not in their natures to
hurry into anything. Now that they had finally discovered their feelings, she hoped they would be able to
work through their problems.

"Doubting her was easily one of the most painful
experiences of my life," Winston admitted quietly.
"Finally, when I couldn't stand it anymore, I laid the
whole thing out in front of her and asked for her side."

"That was risky."

"Yes, she might easily have been offended by my
lack of trust. But to my great relief she didn't take it
that way. Instead she realized what it had cost me to
even broach the subject and rightly took that as an
indication of my commitment to her. She explained the
exact circumstances of what had happened to her in
such a way that I was left with no further concerns
about her integrity."

"I'm very glad to hear that, although not surprised. Any possibility of her involvement in a plot to sabotage the *Silver Zephyr* was farfetched, to say the least."

"Which, sadly, is not the case with Mr. York."

"I'm not convinced of that."

"No, of course you aren't. You're far too loyal and caring a person to accept anything bad about him at this point. But you are also a sensible young woman, so I caution you not to let your heart rule your head. As far as possible, try to view the situation clearly."

"The situation," Allegra protested tightly, "as you call it, amounts to nothing more than some vague warnings and a minor incident which may have absolutely no relation to each other. In point of fact, there may very well be no situation at all."

"I wish I could agree with you, but unfortunately I cannot. Call it instinct, sixth sense, whatever, I have a gut feeling that the *Silver Zephyr* is in danger."

This unequivocal declaration startled Allegra. She could not make light of it, as she would have if it had come from almost anyone other than Winston. His experience and intelligence could not be disregarded. If he thought they were heading into trouble, even if he could not say why or how, his warning had to be heeded.

"If you really believe that," she said carefully, "why is the voyage continuing?"

"Because I don't have the authority to call a halt to it. Only Tristan or the backers can do that."

"Have you mentioned the possibility to them?"

Winston shook his head. "I had intended to bring it up today with Tristan, but that turns out to be impossible. As for the backers . . . I'm hesitant about approaching them.''

Allegra didn't have to ask why. Her own brief exposure to Rutherford had only reinforced all the myths about the movie mogul's inaccessibility, and the run-in with Levinson at the casino, while superficially polite, had carried an undercurrent of anger that disturbed her. As for Charlie Fletcher, he remained a largely unknown quantity.

"How long are you prepared to wait?" she asked.

"It's hard to say. I'm staying in close touch with the hospital, hoping to speak with Tristan as soon as the doctors allow. Short of that, I suppose it would take another incident similar to the engine room fire to make me take action immediately. Or at least,'' he amended dryly, "to try to convince the backers that action is required.''

Since it hardly seemed likely that anything similar to the fire would occur in the few days left to the voyage, Allegra allowed herself to be reassured by that, a brief lapse on the side of wishful thinking which she was shortly to regret.

The morning and early afternoon passed quietly enough. After leaving Paris to the cheers of well-wishers the *Silver Zephyr* wafted south through the Loire Valley in the general direction of the Riviera, which was to be the final stop before beginning the journey home.

Simon and Allegra spent most of the day in the observation lounge, watching the flow of countryside beneath them. They passed over several of the great châteaux where kings had lived and loved. The verdant river valley gave way slowly to the vast plain of the Massif Central. Farms and vineyards slumbered in the soft summer sun.

The great airship was so silent that they were able to hear sounds from the ground below. By propping open the windows they could catch the rush of wind carrying the babble of brooks and the lowing of cattle, along with the heady scent of the ripening earth.

Filled with a rare sense of peacefulness, Allegra could not bring herself to disturb it by mentioning what Winston had told her. Simon was already aware of Tristan's relapse—he had tried to call him earlier—and was clearly worried by it. She did not want to add to his concern with what were, in all likelihood, completely unjustified doubts.

Or at least that was how she rationalized her failure to raise the subject and try for an immediate clearing of the air.

Instead they talked about nothing in particular; movies seen, books read, attitudes toward current fads and trends. All the while they said with the closeness of their bodies and their frequent light touchings all that was really important.

The day passed so pleasantly that Allegra was taken aback to learn, shortly after lunch, that Simon had arranged to go skeet shooting with Charlie Fletcher. She had simply presumed they had no need of other company, while apparently he did.

"You don't mind, do you?" he asked as they made their way toward the portion of the deck set aside for the marksmen, both real and aspiring.

"No, of course not," she assured him, a bit too readily, thinking he would notice her disappointment and find some graceful way to back out. But instead he seemed to take her disclaimer at face value and nodded cheerfully. "You're welcome to join us, if you like."

"I don't shoot."

"There'll be an instructor on hand."

Oh, great. She was supposed to amuse herself taking lessons in something she was guaranteed to hate while he and Charlie indulged their macho tendencies blasting little bits of clay out of the sky.

"No, thanks. I'll just watch."

A stone wall would have picked up on her glumness, but Simon appeared serenely unaware of it. He greeted the boisterous engineer as they both accepted shotguns from a steward.

"You done much shooting?" Charlie inquired, pushing back his cowboy hat and hooking his thumbs into the tailored jeans he wore with a plaid workshirt. He was from Texas, and didn't like to let anyone forget it. Allegra found his forced folksiness grating. She turned away slightly as Simon shrugged.

"Some. It's been awhile."

"Me, too. Be good to get the kinks out."

Beneath the commonplace exchange they were feeling each other out, judging capabilities. There was an instinctive sense of competition between them that piqued Allegra's interest. Maybe watching wouldn't be so boring after all.

The two men were about the same height and size, though Simon was probably five or so years younger than Charlie. The engineer's hair was gray, and his eyes looked red from too much booze or too little sleep, or maybe both. Yet he exuded an unmistakable air of strength and confidence.

The match—that being what it seemed, though no one called it such—began simply enough with a coin toss to see who would go first. Charlie won and grinned as he cocked the weapon at his shoulder.

Addressing the steward who would release the skeets, he said, "I like 'em fast and furious, son, so don't think you have to hold back none."

The young man nodded. His eyes met Allegra's for just an instant, carrying a wealth of stoic tolerance. Then he turned his attention back to the mechanism in front of him.

A quick flip of the spring lever was enough to propel a clay disk out of the chute; it arched high into the sky, where it hung for a moment before beginning to fall. The downward spiral had not yet begun when Charlie fired. The disk shattered, fragments exploding for a radius of several yards. Spent shells dropped to the deck as fresh ones were slipped into position.

Another disk hurtled out, in a different direction and at a slightly varied altitude. The shotgun roared again, and the result was the same.

Ten disks were fired in quick succession, challenging the engineer's reflexes and agility. To the delight of the crowd gathered to watch, he got eight. Only two escaped to fall untouched into the water far below.

As the audience applauded Charlie laughed exuberantly. "Not too bad, if I do say so myself. Always hate to see any get away, though."

"You're pretty handy with that gun," Simon commented as he stepped up to the railing. "I'll bet you've done some time in uniform."

"More than I care to remember."

"See much action?"

"Did a stint in 'Nam. You?"

"The same. *Pull.*" At his command the steward released another disk. It was still climbing along its trajectory when Simon fired, shooting it cleanly from the sky.

He proceeded to do the same again and again, moving with a speed and economy of movement that astonished Allegra. The Texan was an excellent shot, but Simon bested him. All ten of his disks shattered in his sights.

"Well, I'll be . . . ." Charlie murmured, shaking his head in amazement. "If that's how you shoot when you're rusty, I'd hate to see what happens when you get warmed up."

"I guess there are just some things you never forget," Simon said, handing the steward his gun. "What do you say I buy the drinks?"

"Now that's an offer I'd never turn down." Throwing an arm around Simon's shoulders, Charlie beamed a smile in Allegra's direction. "Come on, little lady, we'll wet your whistle and fill your ears with old soldier talk."

Few prospects could have offered less pleasure. Wincing inwardly, she shook her head. "Thanks, but I have some work to do." She glanced at Simon expectantly, thinking that he would surely take the opportunity to bow out and go with her. But instead he merely shrugged.

"That's too bad. If you get done early, come back and join us. We'll probably be here awhile."

While she was struggling with that, Charlie laughed. "I wouldn't be at all surprised. Something tells me we both saw a lot of action." Nodding at Allegra, he opened the door to the bar. "See ya later, little lady."

Simon followed him, casting a glance back over his shoulder. Their eyes met for a moment, hers full of confusion, his dark with something she couldn't quite identify, but which looked surprisingly like regret.

Then he was gone, leaving her to wonder what had happened to all the warm contentment and pleasure in each other's company that seemed to have evaporated without warning, leaving her cold and alone.

Chapter 11

THROUGHOUT THE REST OF THAT AFTERNOON AND into early evening, Allegra tried to convince herself that she was wrong to be hurt by Simon's behavior. It was childish to let anything he did upset her like that. As a grown woman, more than capable of coping with the ups and downs of life, she should be immune. Too bad that she wasn't.

Try though she did, she could not shake the feeling that something was out of kilter. For days Simon had played the part of the perfect lover, coaxing her into intimacy with a mixture of tenderness and passion she could not resist. Now, suddenly, he seemed to prefer swapping war stories with a new acquaintance to spending time with her.

It made no sense. In a halfhearted stab at cynicism, she told herself she should have expected as much.

Everything she had ever believed about the outcome of casual relationships seemed to be coming true. Only in her case, the shipboard romance wasn't even lasting the full extent of the voyage.

Why then did she continue to have faith in Simon and to believe there was some ulterior motive for his sudden interest in Charlie Fletcher? Was she simply trying to shield herself from the unpalatable truth, or did her faith have some basis in reality?

Those questions plagued her all afternoon as she made the rounds of the airship, pausing a dozen times to chat with passengers and assess their reactions to the trip. If their responses were anything to go by, the *Silver Zephyr* was an unqualified success.

Everyone she spoke with exclaimed over the adventure. Though the precise words varied, the main idea was clear: The greatest attraction was the risk-free excitement it offered.

Allegra was gratified to hear the eager responses of such sophisticated men and women, but she was also alert to the implicit meaning behind their praise. Should the *Silver Zephyr*'s safety ever come into doubt, the venture would be destroyed.

She could understand more than ever why Tristan and the backers had decided to ignore the anonymous warnings. So far, at least, their gamble seemed to be paying off.

The voyage was more than half over, and there was no reason to believe the threats had been anything more than the empty rantings of some malcontent. Certainly the fire in the engine room could be dismissed as no more than an accident.

Dressing for dinner, she tried hard not to think beyond the next few days. Once they returned home she might never see Simon again. He had said nothing to indicate he wanted their relationship to continue, and with a continent between them, it would hardly be likely to do so on its own. She would go back to the solitary, work-centered life she had known before and try to forget the brief glimpse he had given her of what might have been.

Her eyes darkened as she glanced at herself in the mirror. She was getting positively maudlin. Her life was good. She had worked hard to achieve everything she had, and had never before been tempted to regret it. For the sake of her sanity, if nothing else, she had to regard Simon as merely a flight of fancy, much like the voyage itself.

She repeated that last part to herself as she dropped a cream lace concoction over her head and slipped her feet into evening sandals. With her hair smoothly coiled at the nape of her neck, she fastened the gold chain set with a single glittering diamond that she had given herself for securing a particularly important account.

Very few women could afford to give themselves such gifts, she reflected as she took a final glance at herself before leaving the cabin. She had every reason to be proud of her hard-won affluence. So why then was she wondering what it would be like to receive such a gift from a man like Simon, given as a symbol of enduring love and commitment?

If she kept on thinking about him like that, her entire evening would be spoiled. Straightening her shoulders in an unconscious gesture of resolve, she joined the crowd streaming toward the cocktail lounge.

It was her intention to find some amicable company to share the half-hour or so until dinner. As she entered the lounge the admiring glances of several men told her that she would have no difficulty.

A wry smile touched her mouth as she realized that in a room full of undeniably attractive, available men, she was still having trouble thinking of anyone except Simon. Confused by her conflicting emotions, she stood hesitantly near the entrance, trying to decide what to do.

Caution advised that she attach herself to one of the numerous groups of people whom she knew and counted, if not as friends, at least as agreeable acquaintances. Pride dictated that she return the discreet signals of any one of the men who would clearly welcome her interest.

She had just about decided that it would do Simon good to arrive and find her with someone else when the choice was suddenly settled for her. A warm, burnished hand lightly touched her arm.

"Sorry I missed you," Simon said. "When I stopped by the cabin you'd already left."

Despite the sudden rush of pleasure through her, she refused to look at him. "Were we supposed to get together this evening? I didn't realize."

His hand tightened slightly, just enough to make her feel compelled to pull away. Freeing herself, she finally gave in to the temptation to look at him.

Like the other men, he was impeccably groomed and dressed in evening clothes. But unlike the others, the veneer of elegance did nothing to hide his essential masculinity.

On the contrary: The black velvet jacket and white silk shirt emphasized the powerful sweep of his chest and shoulders. His hair glinted like hammered gold in the light from the chandeliers, and his pewter eyes held an expression she could not fathom.

He was unmistakably annoyed by her frostiness, but there was also something more. She sensed a conflict within him, as though he were being torn between his desire and his resolve.

In the next instant the expression was gone, replaced by a guarded watchfulness which in its own way was all the more disturbing. There was no animosity in it, only a wariness that suggested he felt she might hurt him. Was he really so vulnerable?

"I'm sorry I left you alone so long," he murmured. "You must not be thinking too well of me."

Her resolve to keep some distance between them was already beginning to slip, prompting her to respond more sharply than she had intended. "I don't have any claim on you, or vice versa. We can both do as we like."

His tanned fingers flexed slightly at his sides. "Is that a fact?"

"I should think it's obvious. After all, we barely know each other."

Her stomach clenched at the sudden flare of his eyes, like tempered steel striking fire. A pulse throbbed in the lean hollow of his cheek. "I've got a news flash for you, lady. We know each other better than a lot of

people who have been married for years. It's damn
hard to keep secrets when you share what we have.''

She swallowed hard, fighting against the sudden
tightness of her throat. ''Hard, but not impossible.''

''What the hell does that mean?''

''Only that there are secrets between us, Simon.
Parts of ourselves we haven't been open about. I can't
pin it down exactly, but I know something is wrong.
And your behavior this afternoon further convinced me
of that.''

He stared at her for a long moment, gauging the full
extent of her distress. Slowly the anger drained out of
him, to be replaced by regret. ''I wish I could insist you
were wrong, but I can't. It's true everything has
happened very quickly between us. There hasn't been
time for a great deal that needs to be said, to be
explained. But there can be time, Allegra, if we only
give ourselves a chance.''

''Time alone isn't enough. We need to trust each
other.'' There, she had said it, had finally given voice
to the thought that had been troubling her all day.

Trust was, for her, an integral part of loving. It had
to be the cornerstone of any relationship they hoped to
have. But it was also, for two such independent people,
profoundly difficult to achieve.

Not for a moment could she pretend that the lack of
trust was all on Simon's side. She was equally guilty.
It was a problem they would have to work out together,
or not at all.

Admitting that, if only inwardly, removed the mental blinders she had been wearing and made her see that

he was every bit as uncertain as she was herself. That crack about them barely knowing each other had hurt him. Determined to make up for it, she slipped her hand into his.

"Let's get a drink, all right?"

As peace offerings went, it wasn't much. But under the circumstances it was the best she could do. A soft sigh of relief escaped her when Simon nodded.

They made their way to the bar in time to get a good spot by the windows. Beneath them, Cannes lay slumbering in the twilight. The steep hillsides of the town were crowded with villas nestled as closely together as the yachts in the harbor below.

A pristine white curve of beach was all but deserted. Beyond lay the cerulean blue expanse of the Mediterranean frothed by drifting sea foam, the dark shadow of night moving slowly across its horizon.

As the last lingering traces of the sun vanished, lights began to blink on one by one until the winding streets were festooned with strings of diamonds rivaling the distant stars. The brief interlude of quiet ended as the population, freshly bathed and bejeweled, began to stream from houses and hotels.

"It looks like a fantasy come to life," Simon mused. "Like something you'd find inside a Fabergé Easter egg."

"Yet it's as real as anything else."

"Is it? Maybe to the people who live here all the time—the waiters, fishermen and so on. But to the visitors, it's a place to forget all about everyday life and indulge in dreams."

"Like the *Silver Zephyr?*"

Allegra set her glass of wine down on the table, aware that her hand shook slightly as she did so. Simon's nearness, the warmth of his big body so close to her own, made the echoes of their recent lovemaking resonate within her. She longed to touch him, to reassure herself that he was part of the real world and not simply a dream.

Uncertain of the wisdom of what she was about to do, yet unable to stop herself, she touched his hand lightly. The contact, minimal though it was, made her tremble.

He looked up, meeting her eyes. "Are you cold?"

"No . . . Simon . . . it isn't easy for me to say this . . . I have the feeling I'm breaking all sorts of rules. But the alternative is to go on playing some sort of elaborate game I don't really understand." She took a deep breath and plunged on. "What I said about us barely knowing each other was true in some ways, but it doesn't change the fact that you've come to mean a great deal to me even in the very short time we've been together. If you hadn't, I would never have made love with you."

"I know that," he said quietly, covering her hand with his own. "You're not the sort of woman to indulge in casual relationships."

"That's right . . . and because I'm that way, I wanted to tell you that after this trip, when we get back home, I'd like to know we were going to find some way to continue seeing each other despite the fact that we live a continent apart."

Simon was silent for what seemed like a long while. As the seconds ticked passed and he did not respond as she had hoped, Allegra's confidence eroded. She had spoken in the conviction that everything they had so far shared indicated that their chance for an enduring relationship was strong. All she wanted was an indication that he felt the same, but it was not forthcoming.

Instead he finally said, "You've also come to mean a great deal to me, more than I can tell you. I want to believe that we can be together back home, but there's so much that's still unsettled. . . ." At the reflexive tightening of her features, he added quickly, "Not with us. Other things you don't know about. Problems I have to straighten out before I can think of making a commitment to another person, or asking for one in return."

Allegra carefully disentangled her hand from his and picked up her glass. The wine was suddenly sour, but she continued to sip it, counting on the pause to steady her at least a little and hide the devastating effect of his words. She hadn't expected any fervent declarations of love, but neither had she thought he would put her off so unflinchingly.

When she could trust herself to speak with some semblance of normality, she murmured, "Don't you think it's a little late to consider that? After all, haven't we already made some sort of promise to each other, if only implicitly?"

Simon stared off into space. The firm line of his jaw was tauter than she had ever seen it, and he seemed to be battling with some private demon that roughened the deep timbre of his voice. "I'm not proud of my behavior with you, Allegra. From the beginning, I knew I was greatly attracted to you, and I was aware of the dangers of getting too close. Saying that I couldn't stay away isn't much of an excuse, but it is the truth.''

''Are you always so susceptible to women you don't plan to see again?''

Beneath his burnished tan, his cheeks reddened slightly. ''I didn't say that. You're twisting my words. We've met under unusual circumstances. It stands to reason that there should be problems, not necessarily between us, but between our pasts and any future we may be able to make together. Neither one of us is a blank slate.''

''I never thought you were. But I also hadn't imagined you were so involved that you wouldn't even be willing to plan on us seeing each other again.''

''If I considered only myself, I wouldn't hesitate for a moment about arranging to see you back in the States. But I told you, there are complications that need to be worked out.''

Complications. What did that mean? At the moment, only one possibility occurred to her. ''Are you . . . involved with another woman?''

Simon's hands tightened on the sides of his chair. He stared at her in surprise that gave way to anger. ''Is that what you really think of me? That I would be capable of such deceit?''

''Would it be deceit?'' she countered. ''You're away from home, among strangers. Other men—and women —feel free in such circumstances to indulge themselves in ways that would ordinarily be impossible.''

''Is that an impersonal observation,'' he demanded scathingly, ''or a statement of your own values?''

"Of course it has nothing to do with me! I'm not the one who's backing off from a commitment."

"Maybe not. But you are pushing me up against a wall. Why is that necessary?"

"Because I , . ." Allegra broke off, skidding to a halt against her own unruly thoughts. Why was she doing this? She had nothing to gain and everything to lose by pushing Simon. He was not a man to be nagged or cajoled into anything he didn't want to do. And she was not a woman to attempt such a ploy. Pride alone was enough to stop her.

To tell him again that she had come to care for him would do no good. She would have to take the next step and admit that her feelings ran deeper than any she had ever before experienced, but that was too intensely personal a revelation to make to a man who had just informed her that he was unprepared to offer any commitment.

"Never mind," she said at last. "I shouldn't have brought this up in the first place. Let's just forget it."

Something of the pain she was feeling must have reached him, for he leaned closer, touching her cheek gently with a callused finger. "I have no intention of forgetting it. You're far too important to me." Ruefully he added, "If you weren't, you wouldn't be able to rile me so easily."

"I meant to," she said candidly. "After you went off with Charlie, I was hurt enough to want to get back at you."

"Sweetheart, about Charlie . . ."

Whatever Simon had intended to say was lost as Winston suddenly appeared at their side, his face grim and his eyes dark with anger. Allegra looked up at him in surprise. She had never before seen his innate reserve so severely dented.

"I'm sorry to interrupt, but something rather serious has happened. If you would excuse us, Mr. York . . ."

As Allegra instinctively started to rise to go with him, Simon also stood. Quietly, but with unmistakable firmness, he said, "You'll have to fill me in, too, Captain."

Winston balked at that but could find no way to get rid of him without causing a scene. Reluctantly he nodded. "All right, but not here. Let's step outside."

The corridor adjacent to the cocktail lounge was empty. Winston glanced around carefully before he said, "One of my crew has been injured trying to repair a jammed valve on a ballast tank. It came off in his hand, releasing thousands of pounds of helium in a jet that flattened him against a bulkhead. He's in medical now with a broken leg and several fractured ribs."

"And the tank? Is it still leaking?" Simon demanded.

"No, fortunately the crew that was on hand at the time was able to make emergency repairs. But if the leak had continued for even a few more minutes, you would certainly have felt it up here. We would have begun to lose altitude."

"Is there a possibility this wasn't an accident?" Allegra asked.

"More than that. When I got back to my office I found another note." He pulled a piece of paper from his shirt pocket and handed it to them. It was similar to the one Arthur Rutherford had found on his breakfast tray; the message was written in block letters on the *Silver Zephyr's* own stationery.

I'M THROUGH WAITING. CANCEL THE REST OF THE TRIP NOW OR A JAMMED RELEASE VALVE WILL BE THE LEAST OF YOUR PROBLEMS.

"Seems pretty clear," Simon muttered. "Whoever's responsible for injuring the crewman doesn't intend to stop there."

"Was anyone seen going into or coming out of your office who didn't have business there?" Allegra asked.

Winston shook his head. "Unfortunately not. The bridge watch were all busy with their duties. No one noticed a thing."

They were silent for a moment as several passengers went by, then Simon asked, "Do you have any idea how long ago the note might have been left?"

"I left an hour ago to dress for dinner, so the office was empty from then on. There was a shift change shortly thereafter, when the night watch came on. For a few minutes twice as many people as usual would have been on the bridge. That might have been when our mysterious visitor slipped in."

"Makes sense, but we're still no closer to figuring out who's responsible."

"Have you told anyone else?" Allegra asked.

"No, but I don't think we can keep this from the backers. They have a right to know."

"So does Tristan," Simon pointed out.

"I agree. But when I tried to contact him a few

minutes ago at the hospital, I was informed that he is still very dazed and cannot be disturbed.''

"Then I must insist on being present when you inform the backers.''

"In what capacity?''

"To represent Tristan's interests, as he asked me to do when I agreed to make this trip in his place.''

Winston thought that over for a moment before reluctantly agreeing. "All right, but I don't expect the others to like it.''

They didn't, but Arthur Rutherford, Bertrand Levinson and Charlie Fletcher were too caught up in the crisis suddenly confronting them to offer more than perfunctory objections to Simon's presence.

"I don't know why you have to be involved,'' Arthur Rutherford said, "but it's not worth fighting about.'' Gesturing to the note being passed around, he added, "That's what we've got to worry about.''

"Just what we need,'' Charlie Fletcher muttered. "Some nut on our tail.''

"Don't write this guy off as a crazy,'' Bernard Levinson insisted. "So far his behavior has been very clever. He's slowly accelerated our awareness of him without revealing anything about himself.''

"Anything except that he wants to destroy the *Silver Zephyr*,'' Winston said.

Allegra shifted slightly in her chair, regarding the men. "Actually, I don't think whoever's behind this does want to destroy the vessel. He seems anxious to stop short of that by curtailing the voyage.''

"Which amounts to the same thing as destruction,'' Rutherford pointed out, taking a puff on his cigar. "If we cancel the remainder of the trip, no matter what reason we give, we'll raise the specter of the *Hindenburg* all over again. Our claims to being completely safe and reliable will be finished, and we might as well bag the whole project.''

Levinson agreed. "We can say good-bye to our investment, not to mention any profit.''

As she listened to the men Allegra was becoming increasingly impatient. Finally she could contain herself no longer. "It seems to me that our priorities need some adjusting. There are hundreds of lives at stake. Surely that's far more important than any monetary consideration?''

Fletcher leaned back against the overstuffed leather chair and eyed her tolerantly. "'Course we care about the passengers, honey, but we don't want to get carried away here. Overreacting won't do anyone any good.''

"After all,'' Rutherford pointed out, "we have no indication that whoever's behind this actually has the capacity to harm the passengers. Injuring one crewman is a long way from threatening hundreds of lives.''

Simon had remained silent since the meeting began, but now at last he spoke. Very quietly, so that they had to lean forward to hear him, he said, "You're trying to rationalize your way out of a very painful decision. I can sympathize with that, but the fact is, whoever jammed that release valve is very familiar with the engineering systems of this vessel. He knew exactly how to set up a situation that would result in injury.' We were very lucky to get off as lightly as we did. Under the circumstances, I have no doubt that Tristan would want the rest of the trip canceled.''

"That's very impressive," Rutherford muttered, "but hardly to the point. You have no authority here."

Before Simon could reply, Winston stepped forward. "Perhaps not, but I do, and I agree with Mr. York. The voyage should be stopped."

The backers exchanged wary looks. It was clear that Levinson spoke for them all as he said, "We all value your services as captain, but you are not irreplaceable. If you find yourself unable to continue the voyage, command will be turned over to the next senior officer. If he refuses, we'll keep on until we find an alternative. One way or the other, this venture will continue."

In the harsh silence that followed Allegra recognized that battle lines were being drawn. She, Simon and Winston were on one side, with the backers on the other. Such a division could only work against them all.

Attempting to effect a compromise, she said, "Nobody wants to give in to blackmail, but we have to consider the risk to the passengers. By tomorrow we'll be back out over the Atlantic. Another incident like the jammed valve could result in tragedy. Surely you don't want that."

"Of course not," Levinson snapped. "Keep in mind that none of us has proposed leaving the vessel. We'll be just as much at risk as everyone else. But I'll be damned if I'll give in to this nut, whoever he is."

"I'll go along with that," Rutherford said. "Our saboteur may know his way around this ship, but he still strikes me as an amateur. He hasn't made any demands or given any indication of why he wants to stop the voyage."

"That's what's bothered me about this from the beginning," Simon admitted. "I could understand an attempt at extortion: Pay 'x' amount of money or risk the worst. But there hasn't been anything like that. We're left in the dark as to this guy's motives."

"Which is undoubtedly the point," Fletcher said. "We're dealing with someone who's sufficiently skillful not to give any clues as to his identity. Let's not make the mistake of underrating him."

"If you really believe that," Winston interjected, "then you should be in favor of stopping the trip, at least temporarily, while we sort this out."

"I didn't say that. There's too much to lose."

Simon shook his head angrily. "No one has more at stake than Tristan. The *Silver Zephyr* is his dream. Years of his life and every cent he could get his hands on went into it. Yet I know if he were here, he would insist that we not take chances with anyone's life."

"But he isn't here," Fletcher pointed out. "As a matter of fact, Tristan is the only person closely involved in this venture who didn't make the trip." Glancing from one to the other, he murmured, "Strikes me as kind of peculiar, under the circumstances."

A light flared deep within Simon's eyes. Tautly he demanded, "What exactly are you suggesting, Charlie?"

The Texan shrugged lightly. "I'm just making a comment, is all. Maybe Tristan really does stand to lose everything if this project fails. But what if that isn't so? What if he's protected somehow and would actually come out better if the *Silver Zephyr* didn't make it?"

"How the hell could he do that?"

"Your guess is as good as mine. All I know is that he isn't here and we are."

Allegra had heard enough. She was not about to sit by and let her friend be libeled like that. "Tristan is thousands of miles away, Mr. Fletcher. How do you imagine he could be behind what's been happening?"

The others nodded, struck by the telling inconsistency in his argument. But Charlie did not look at all concerned. Instead he merely said, "Simple enough, little lady. He'd have to have somebody on board who was working for him."

The words hung in the air as slowly, irresistibly, all eyes fastened on Simon.

Chapter 12

"ARE YOU SERIOUSLY SUGGESTING I'M RESPONSIBLE for what's been happening, Charlie?" Simon asked quietly. He had not moved from his position on the couch, but Allegra was not fooled by his apparent calm. She saw the anger in his silvery eyes and sensed the tight rein he was keeping on his temper.

"You tell me, fella. All I know is that you seem to be around whenever there's trouble. Weren't you in the engine room when that fire broke out? And how about this evening? Care to tell us what you were doing about the time that note was being left?"

"I was changing for dinner."

"Alone?"

The watchful eyes switched to Allegra. Under their scrutiny, she blushed. She hadn't expected her relationship with Simon to be a secret, but neither did she relish the thought of it being dragged out for examination by these men.

"Ease off, Fletcher," Simon growled. "You're treading a dangerous line."

"So the little lady can't give you an alibi. Too bad. From that chat we had this afternoon, I'd say you're more than capable of planning something like this."

"That's an extremely serious accusation," Winston snapped. "I suggest you watch yourself. Libel is a nasty crime."

"So is sabotage," Rutherford retorted. "Besides, no one is saying Mr. York is responsible for the problems we've been having. All that's being suggested is that he is a potential suspect, possibly through no fault of his own." Glancing at the other backers, he went on, "We have to be realistic about this. Since we want the voyage to continue, it has to be under the safest possible conditions."

"What's that supposed to mean?" Allegra demanded. She was infuriated by their attack, recognizing it as the desperate ploy of men determined to have their own way at any cost. By pinning suspicion on Simon, they could claim that the crisis had effectively been defused and that there was no reason not to go on with the trip.

Bertrand Levinson stood up, heading for Winston's desk. "I believe what Arthur means is that we owe it to both ourselves and the passengers to take sensible precautions. Pending some confirmation of Mr. York's identity . . ." he reached for the phone . . . "and some explanation for the recent events . . ." he punched out a number . . . "it would be prudent for

Mr. York to agree to remain in his cabin.'' Speaking into the receiver, he said, ''Give me security, please.''

''This is preposterous!'' Winston exclaimed. ''You can't expect me to sit by and allow a passenger to be incarcerated without due process.''

''You can do anything you like,'' Levinson said. ''But keep in mind what you've already been told: You're not indispensable. With or without your approval, Mr. York is going to spend some time on ice.''

Turning his attention back to the phone, he said, ''Send somebody up here who can install a lock.''

''You have no authority to do this,'' Allegra protested. ''There has to be some alternative.''

Charlie Fletcher shrugged. ''I can think of only one: If York doesn't want to cool his heels in his cabin, he can agree to leave the *Silver Zephyr* immediately.''

Allegra's hazel eyes darkened. She realized the logic of what the Texan was suggesting. How could Simon fail to agree when the alternative was to be locked up in his cabin, possibly for the rest of the voyage? Dreading the thought of being separated from him so suddenly, she was both relieved and astonished when he shook his head firmly.

''No, thanks. I'll remain on board.'' White teeth were bared in a humorless grin. ''If you gentlemen really believe I'm responsible for the sabotage, then by all means lock me up.''

His unexpected acquiescence took them aback. Rutherford coughed and loosened his tie. ''Very sensible of you to take this attitude, York. Saves us all a lot of trouble.''

"We'll try to get it cleared up quickly," Levinson promised.

"It won't be so bad," Charlie chimed in. "Beats those tiger cages in 'Nam."

"I'm overwhelmed by my good fortune," Simon muttered dryly. His expression was unreadable as he met Allegra's worried eyes. She thought he would say something to her, offer some explanation for his docility, but apparently he thought better of it. His mouth tightened in a grim line as he abruptly left the office, accompanied by the backers and the puzzled locksmith.

When they were alone Winston muttered a sharp, blunt curse. "This is the damnedest situation I've ever been in. Those men are behaving outrageously, yet Simon seems willing to go along with them."

"I did think he'd protest more vehemently," Allegra agreed. She was deeply puzzled by his behavior. He seemed not at all upset by the outrage being perpetrated against him.

For just a moment she considered the possibility that his lack of surprise stemmed from guilt. Then she firmly, utterly rejected that thought. Simon was no more responsible for the sabotage than she was. There had to be some other explanation for his willingness to remain on board under conditions that were nothing short of insulting.

In the instant before he left, she had glimpsed something in him . . . resolution, comprehension, confirmation . . . something. As though a light had suddenly gone on in his mind.

But if that were the case, if he had put the pieces together and realized the identity of the culprit, why hadn't he spoken up? Such knowledge would do no good if he remained locked in his cabin.

Silently she tried to follow the thought processes that might have led him to accept incarceration as the price of remaining on board. The confrontation with the backers had crystallized a suspicion that had been forming in her mind since she first learned of the potential danger to the *Silver Zephyr*. Everything that had happened since then confirmed the probability that the saboteur was not just some random nut, but someone with an insider's knowledge of the vessel, and a motive, however twisted, for threatening it.

Eliminating Simon, which she did unhesitatingly, meant that the most likely suspects were the backers themselves. It didn't stand to reason that three such disparate men could be acting in concert. She had to narrow the field to one.

The simplest way to do that was to wait until Simon was alone, convince security to let her into his room, and ask him straight out. But she couldn't do that. If she went to him now, she would make her loyalties crystal clear and alert the saboteur to the fact that she was another problem he needed to take care of.

Before that could happen she intended to find out once and for all what possible end might be served by the *Silver Zephyr*'s destruction.

"Winston," she said slowly, "I've got a few things to take care of. . . . I'll see you later."

As she rose to leave he frowned. "You're very calm about all this."

"Is that how I seem? It's misleading, but let's hope others think so, too."

"What do you mean?"

She smiled gently. "Never mind. Believe me, the moment I find anything out for sure, you'll hear about it. In the meantime, do you think you could arrange to delay our departure?"

"You can count on it." His eyes flashed grimly. "Those 'gentlemen'—I use the word loosely—who just left may think they run things around here, but they are mistaken. There's no way I'll let this ship be caught over the Atlantic with a saboteur on board."

"Good." Her hand was on the doorknob when she glanced back at him over her shoulder. "Think about what you just said, Winston. Unless our saboteur has a death wish, he's not going to stick around for the final scene. I suggest you keep a close eye on anyone going ashore."

His startled agreement was almost enough to make her laugh. Almost, but not quite. Her expression was serious as she hurried down the corridor toward the communications room.

Making contact with New York proved more difficult than she had anticipated. It was going on 3:00 A.M. there, and the friend she was calling took awhile to answer. When Cassia Jones finally came on the other end, Allegra apologized profusely for disturbing her.

"I'm awfully sorry, Cass, but I've got a real problem, and I'm hoping you can help."

"Why is it I'm not surprised to hear from you?" her friend murmured groggily. At twenty-seven, a scant half-year younger than Allegra, Cassia was a stunning silver-blonde whose willowy body and angelic beauty literally made men walk into walls. Mother Nature had truly outdone herself by planting within that gorgeous form the mind of a certified genius.

Cassia was brilliant in a way very few people could ever fully grasp. She moved through life in a pleasant fog of her own ruminations, surfacing every so often with some breakthrough that caused the lesser mortals at the think tank where she worked to gasp in mingled astonishment and envy.

Her beauty and the effect it had on others left her completely unmoved. She was genuinely oblivious to it, which perhaps was just as well. For behind that dazzling intellect and magnificent body were the heart and soul of a true softie.

Cassia was, simply put, the nicest person Allegra had ever met. She would do anything for her friends, including using her extraordinary resources to ferret out information.

"I know you thought I was nuts to go on this trip," Allegra admitted, "and I'm beginning to think you weren't completely wrong."

"What's happened?" All remnants of sleep were gone as Cassia swiftly turned her remarkable mind to the problem at hand. Allegra could picture her in her apartment at the renowned Center for Advanced Studies where she both lived and worked.

Despite her brilliance, or perhaps because of it, Cassia had yet to dip a toe into the uneasy waters of male-female relationships. She seemed to think she was immune. Allegra knew better, judging her more than ready to fall in head first once she met the right man. But that was another issue for another time.

"We have a problem here." Briefly she outlined the events of the last few days, ending with the injury to the crewman and the second note.

Cassia listened without interrupting. When Allegra finished, her friend was silent for a moment before she said, "How old is Simon York?"

"Thirty-five, but what's that got to do with anything?"

"He's not married, is he? No, of course he isn't, or you wouldn't be so involved."

Allegra flushed. She had deliberately omitted any mention of her relationship with Simon to refrain from prejudicing Cassia, but it seemed she hadn't been clever enough. Not bothering to deny what was apparently obvious to her perspicacious friend, she got on with it.

"It's not Simon I'm worried about. I need to pin down a motive if I'm going to have any chance of discovering who's responsible."

"The motive's easy," Cassia announced. "It's money."

"How can you be sure?"

"It's a matter of deductive reasoning. There are only a very limited range of causes for negative human behavior: greed, lust, insanity. Since it seems we can eliminate the last two, we're left with the first."

"But if this feeling I have about one of the backers being responsible is correct, that doesn't make any sense. They'd all lose money, not make it."

"Haven't you ever heard of insurance?"

"W-what . . . ?"

"It's not as outlandish as you might think. What was to stop one of the backers from taking out a hefty insurance policy for more than he'd invested and then trying to make sure he could cash it in?"

"Who would underwrite something like that?"

"Any number of companies, starting with Lloyds of London. You can insure pretty much anything if you're willing to pay the premiums. For the *Silver Zephyr* they probably weren't even all that steep. As outlandish as that overgrown balloon seems, it really is safe."

"We do have insurance, of course," Allegra said thoughtfully. "There were inspectors from the company all over the ship during our shakedown cruise."

"That's what I figured. My guess is that the saboteur had a pretty easy time getting a policy limited to the maiden voyage and payable if the trip wasn't completed for any reason other than outright negligence on the part of the owners."

"Which would explain why he's so desperate to stop us before we can return to New York," Allegra said.

"Exactly. Now all you need to know is whether or not such a policy actually exists, and if it does, who benefits."

"Can you find that out?"

"Of course," Cassia said, sounding slightly miffed that Allegra could have entertained even the slightest doubt. "I'll just get on the computer and run it down."

"I realize you're a whiz with that thing, but I don't understand how you can use it to find out the kind of information I need."

"It's simple. You just have to be hooked up to the right big computers, which I happen to be."

Allegra knew better than to question her any further. Some of the projects Cassia worked on at the think tank were most definitely classified. With the contribution she made to national security, it was reasonable that she would be able to get any facts and figures she needed without a whole lot of fuss.

"When will you be in touch?"

"Half an hour or so."

Hanging up, Allegra steeled herself to do nothing for the next thirty minutes. It was even harder than she'd expected. After pouring herself a cup of thick, tepid coffee from the communal pot, she wandered around, staring at the various screens and dials, and trying to stay out of the way of the night crew.

The two men and one woman monitoring the panoply of equipment glanced at her occasionally, but no one said anything. They put up with her anxious presence tolerantly, yet there was an undeniable sense of relief in the room when Cassia at last called back.

"I've got it," her friend exclaimed, clearly pleased. "He didn't even cover his tracks well."

"He who?"

Cassia told her. It took a moment to sink in. When it did, Allegra's eyes flashed, and her mouth tightened grimly. "I should have guessed. Thanks a million. I'll let you know how it works out."

"Wait a sec. What are you going to do?"

"Why, expose him, of course."

"You can't handle this alone. You've got to call the authorities."

"There may not be time. I've got to go. But don't worry, I'll get back to you as soon as I can." Before Cassia could object further, Allegra hung up and hurried out of the communications room.

As she dashed down the corridor she quickly decided on a course of action. She had to free Simon, then find Winston, alert security, start a search of the aircraft. . . .

She had barely begun to implement those plans when they showed every sign of disintegrating. To start with, Simon wasn't in his cabin. The young steward who undid the newly added bolt and opened the door turned gray when he realized the prisoner was gone. "I don't understand. . . . He couldn't have gotten out. . . ."

Allegra stood in the center of the stateroom, looking around. The signs of Simon's presence were unmistakable. His suede jacket lay over the back of a chair. A tie she recognized was tossed on the foot of the bed. The faint scent of his spicy aftershave teased her nose. He had been there very recently.

There was only one door to the stateroom, and that had been locked from the outside. The large plate glass windows were sealed shut. So how had he escaped?

She was growing more baffled with each passing moment when at last her eyes lit on the grill of the ventilation duct set high up near the ceiling. It was not quite flush with the wall. Closer inspection revealed that the four small screws holding it in place had been removed.

Allegra shook her head in amazement. Simon was a big man; he must have just barely made it through the opening. Beyond the grill, the duct opened up to about three feet in height and two in width. Large enough for a very determined man to make his way along.

The conduits for the ventilation system ran to every part of the ship. He could be anywhere. She smothered a groan of frustration and turned back to the steward. "I'm going down to the hold. Please find the captain immediately and ask him to join me there. It's very important."

Without waiting for a response she hurried off. Every step she took, every second that ticked past, reminded her that there might be very little time left.

Only she and Winston knew that the *Silver Zephyr* would not make its scheduled night departure from Cannes within the hour. The saboteur must still believe he had only until then to complete his preparations and manage his escape.

Choosing which hold to search was simply a guess. She had a layperson's understanding of the vessel's engineering systems, enough to know that its most vulnerable points were the helium tanks. Although the gas was nonflammable, any sudden loss of pressure could send the *Silver Zephyr* into a death spiral.

Unless she was very much mistaken, the only way to achieve complete destruction of the craft would be to plant a bomb near the tanks, with a timing mechanism set to go off after the saboteur was safely back on land.

Now that the pieces were falling together, she realized that from the beginning the only logical suspects had been the backers. Everyone else's luggage had been carefully searched, but the men whose money had financed the venture were given the courtesy of sending their belongings on board without inspection.

Knowing what to look for did not make her search any easier. The helium tanks were immense, several stories in height and surrounded by girders that offered numerous hiding places.

After kicking off her high-heeled shoes, she began to climb. The long skirt of her lace dress caught around her ankles. She hiked it up with one hand as the other gripped the narrow railing of the rickety stairs.

Some twenty feet above the floor she paused to catch her breath and look around. The tops of the tanks were within sight above her. Nearby was a catwalk that ran the full circumference of the hold. If she could make it that far, she would have a good view of the entire area.

Her feet were hurting from the bare metal grid, and her breath came in labored rasps before she finally reached her goal. She levered herself up the last few inches, then slumped against the wall and closed her eyes for an instant.

Although heights had never before bothered her, she was feeling undeniably dizzy. Every instinct she possessed for self-preservation was screaming at her to flee, yet she could not. Held in the grip of danger greater than any she had ever known, she found herself unable to move.

But not for long. A sound farther down the ledge where the shadow of one of the tanks obscured the light suddenly alerted her to the fact that she was not alone. Her eyes flew open, straining through the dimness. At first she could make out nothing.

Almost convinced that she had imagined the sound, she was about to go on when a flicker of motion froze her in place. She pressed back against the wall, hardly daring to breathe.

A shape moved out of the shadows. Allegra blinked hard, willing it to vanish. It did not. Instead it loomed closer, revealing itself to be very large, unmistakably male, and heading straight toward her.

Chapter 13

"WHAT THE HELL ARE YOU DOING HERE?" SIMON grated, his hands digging into her arms. With a muttered curse he swung her off her feet and into the shadows.

Before she could answer he pushed her closer to the bulkhead, his big body hard against her own. "Be quiet," he muttered tightly. "Someone's coming."

Unable to see over or around him, she had to take his word for it. The cold metal pressing into her back made her tremble, but no more so than his nearness. Her intense awareness of him overrode even her fear. A soft sigh escaped her as she nestled closer, resting her head on his broad chest just above his heart.

"It must not have been anything after all," he murmured thickly a few minutes later when the sound was not repeated. Stepping back, he grasped her chin and forced her to look at him.

"Now, answer my question: What are you doing here?"

Still caught up in the heady sense of his nearness, Allegra looked at him blankly before recollection flooded back. Her eyes widened as she gasped, "Oh, Simon, thank heavens, I found you! When I went to your room and discovered you were gone, I couldn't begin to think where you might be."

"Why did you want to see me?" he asked, his expression suddenly shuttered and unfathomable.

"I had to tell you . . . I found out . . . after they took you back to the cabin, I realized . . ." She broke off, drawing a breath. This was no time to be rattling on, making no sense, while precious seconds were lost.

About to continue, hopefully on a more rational note, she was interrupted when Simon held up a peremptory hand. "Never mind. I can guess what you're trying to say. This isn't the time or the place to listen to your suspicions. There's just too much that's going to happen too soon."

"No, you don't understand. I really do know. You've got to—"

"There's only one thing I've got to do: get you out of here before the saboteur acts. We've no time to waste, Allegra. So just do as I say."

"I won't! You can't make me go anywhere. How you could even think that I'd . . ."

Again his big hands bit into her arms, this time with

desperation. "Allegra, I know you don't trust me, but you've got to take my word for this. Until I can figure out who the saboteur is—"

"But I told you, I know who he is! Listen to me. . . ."

"You should take the little lady's advice, York. She's a step ahead of you."

Simon whirled around, keeping his body between Allegra and the man who had suddenly appeared on the catwalk. She could feel the feral tension radiating from him as he faced their adversary.

With no hint of surprise or fear, he murmured, "So it was you, Fletcher. Nice to have my suspicions confirmed."

"Enjoy it while you can. Neither one of you is going to be around much longer."

"Oh, come on," Simon sneered. "You can't be that stupid."

The Texan flushed, his weathered skin turning an ugly red. He shifted the .45 automatic in his hand. "Watch yourself, old boy. This ain't some dumb skeet shoot. You're up against the real thing."

"Funny," Simon drawled mockingly, "all I see is some stupid bastard who got in over his head and panicked."

A low growl broke from Fletcher. He took a step forward. "Shut up! I don't have to listen to you."

Allegra glanced frantically from one man to the other. What was Simon doing? Charlie seemed barely in control of himself as it was. A few more taunts and he would be pushed over the edge.

"Don't you mean you're afraid to listen? How does it feel to know you're headed for prison, or worse? Must be pretty hard on a man who doesn't give a damn about anything except himself."

"You don't know what you're talking about! I figured this operation down to the second. There's no way I'll be stopped."

"You're lying to yourself, Charlie. Think about it; nothing's gone right for you. Your threats were ignored, and you've been pushed into a corner. You even had to agree with Rutherford and Levinson to keep the *Silver Zephyr* in the air."

His confidence undented, the Texan smiled humorlessly. "And they fell for it. Nobody knows I'm behind what's been happening except you and the little lady. And you don't count, 'cause I'm going to be taking care of both of you real soon." He straightened his shoulders, his grip tightening on the .45. "That's enough talking. Get moving."

Allegra was tempted to obey, if only to gain them a few more minutes. But Simon refused to budge. "Why should we?" he demanded. "If you really plan to shoot us, do it here."

Fletcher's mouth hardened to a thin, ugly line. "I'm warning you, move or I'll take you both out right now."

Simon stepped forward, interposing himself between Allegra and the gun before she had a chance to realize what was happening. About to protest, she caught herself just in time. The last thing Simon needed was a distraction, no matter how well meant.

Taking a step closer to the Texan, he said quietly, "Think about what you're saying. There's no silencer on that gun. By this time, someone will have noticed I'm not in my stateroom and they'll be searching for me. The second you fire, security guards will be all over you. Besides, what happens if you hit one of the tanks? We're a hundred feet off the ground. If we lose buoyancy now, we'll go down like a stone. Chances are you and just about everyone else will be killed."

"You talk too much, York. I'm not going to miss, and as for the security guards, this is a damn big hold, with plenty of places to hide. They won't find me in time."

"Are you sure you were a marine?" Simon asked. "You don't act like one. Any raw recruit could tell you the logistics of this operation stink." He looked the other man up and down with blatant derision. "Those stories you told me about being in 'Nam must have been fairy tales. Best you probably ever saw was desk duty."

"*Why you . . .*" Fletcher released the safety on the gun just as Simon took another step toward him. Barely six feet separated them. The Texan had a clear shot; it would be impossible for him to miss.

White with fear, Allegra began to shake uncontrollably. She was an instant away from seeing the man she loved killed before her eyes.

Loved? There was no time to question that realization, no chance to reflect on what it meant. Nothing mattered but the absolute certainty that she cherished

him heart and soul, and that if he were hurt, a vital part
of herself would die.

A scream rose in her throat. She struggled desperately to hold it back, but could not. A red mist of anguish
gripped her as she cried out in rejection of all that was
about to happen. *"No!"*

The tormented sound echoed off the walls of the hold
like the ancient keening of mourners. Startled, Fletcher
shifted his glance back to her. In the second that his
attention was distracted, Simon acted. He sprang with
the concentrated force of a huge hunting cat, hurling
himself across the space separating them and throwing
the full force of his weight and strength against the
other man.

They fell across the catwalk, the gun falling from
Fletcher's hand and clattering to the floor. For long,
seemingly endless moments, the two men fought to
reach it. They were well matched in both size and
ability, and the outcome might have continued in doubt
had Allegra not tried to take matters into her own
hands.

Steeling herself, she moved cautiously around the
struggling figures, maneuvering to reach the gun. It
was almost within her grasp when the Texan suddenly
became aware of what she was doing and moved to take
advantage of it.

A large hand lashed out to grab her ankle. Allegra
cried out and tried to jerk away, but could not. He
pulled hard, knocking her off balance and sending her
crashing to the ground.

Fear for her safety made Simon forget himself just

long enough for Fletcher to break free of his grip. Clasping both fists together, he thrust upward with a bone-crunching blow that sent Simon reeling against the bulkhead.

Realizing what was about to happen, Allegra scrambled frantically for the gun, but she was not in time. Fletcher got to the weapon first, pointing it at them with deadly accuracy.

"All right," he muttered through clenched teeth, "you made your try and it didn't work. Now move, or by God, I'll shoot."

There was no reason to doubt him. The rage in his eyes bordered on madness. Simon stood up dazedly, holding the back of his head as Allegra slipped his arm around her shoulders.

She was close to tears at the folly of her own actions, but refused to let them fall. Later there might be time for self-recrimination, just then there was only the silent, inward ticking of a clock that warned them that their chance of escape—indeed, of survival—was running out.

At Fletcher's prodding they made their way down the catwalk to a small utility room full of fuse boxes and pipes. Allegra recognized it as one of the several points throughout the vessel where maintenance workers could get access to vital systems.

That meant there was a steady coming and going of crew members in the area, but only during the day shift. At night no one would come near the place unless there was an emergency.

"Get your hands up, York," Charlie ordered. As Simon reluctantly obeyed the Texan pulled a pair of handcuffs from his back pocket and tossed them at Allegra. "Fasten him to that overhead pipe."

She wanted to refuse, but a single cautionary look from Simon warned her of the danger of doing so. Reluctantly she stood on tiptoe to secure the handcuffs around his wrists.

As she stepped back Charlie leveled the gun on her. "You're next, little lady." He chuckled callously. "I sure do hate to leave a pretty filly in such a fix, but there's just no option. Get your arms up, honey."

Allegra obeyed slowly. With her hands around the overhead pipe, she had to stretch to keep even her toes on the ground. Her breasts thrust upward, pressing against the thin lace of her gown.

Fletcher eyed her appreciatively. With one hand he secured the cuffs as the other continued to hold the gun on her. "Yes, sir, sure is a shame. You're a damn good-lookin' woman."

As the clasp clicked into place he stepped back, surveying her with blatant enjoyment. Rich brown hair streaked by the sun tumbled around her shoulders. Her face was pale, its whiteness offset by the glitter of her hazel eyes and the deep rose of lips she had bitten in her anxiety.

Her extreme helplessness held a certain sensuality for a man of Fletcher's violent temperament. It was obvious from the way he was looking at her that he genuinely regretted the lack of an opportunity to enjoy her more fully.

"Believe me, honey, I hate to leave you like this. But there just ain't no choice."

A moment later she saw what he meant. He slipped a hand into the pocket of his jacket and removed a small bundle from which several wires extruded. From another pocket came a timing device, no more sophisticated than what could be found in many kitchens, yet perfectly adequate for the task at hand.

Holding the bundle up, he taunted Simon. "Remember this, York? Good old *plastique*, just like we used in 'Nam. There's enough here to take out a couple of fair-sized factories and at least half a dozen barracks. I figure the explosives will shatter the helium tanks and a chunk of the fuselage. You'll lose pressure in seconds and plummet straight down."

Allegra watched in horror as he adroitly connected the timing device and set it. Where there had been silence there was now a low, steady ticking.

"Should be a hell of a ride," Fletcher laughed. "Almost hate to miss it. But at least I'll have a good view from the ground."

"How do you plan to explain your survival to the insurance company?" Simon asked swiftly. "They're going to be a bit curious."

Fletcher shrugged. "That's the beauty of having this happen while the *Silver Zephyr* is moored. Once I hit the ground, I'll head for the nearest telephone. As far as the insurance company will know, I'm all upset about the latest warning and disagree with the decision of the others to keep quiet about it. I think something terrible's about to happen and want to know what to do. They'll tell me to contact the authorities right away, and I'll be happy to oblige. But by then it'll be too late."

Allegra hated to admit it, but his plan made a twisted sort of sense. Even if anyone present at the meeting in Winston's office survived, it would simply be his word against Fletcher's. And there would be the compelling evidence of his cooperation with the authorities to offset any charges made against him.

He'd walk away free and clear, with a huge amount of money, while the rest of them . . .

That didn't bear thinking about. In an effort to distract herself as much as gain some time, she asked softly, "What made you do this, Charlie?"

"Sheer survival, honey. I'm up to my neck in debt, with no other way out."

"There's always the legal refuge of bankruptcy. You'd be protected. . . ."

He laughed harshly. "The guys I owe wouldn't go for anything like that. You either pay the money or they take it out of your hide." He shrugged, as though the question of motive were really of very little interest to him. "It's too bad it had to be this way, but those are the breaks." Glancing at the timer, he added, "Much as I enjoy your company, I'll be leaving now."

"You won't make it," Simon warned. "You'll be stopped the moment you try to get off the ship."

Fletcher cast him a chiding look as he eased the door open. "I don't exactly plan to go out the front way. These mooring ropes are fine for sliding down, especially for an old paratrooper like me."

On that note he threw a mocking salute and vanished from their sight. For several moments they could hear his footsteps hastening along the catwalk. Then there was silence, punctured only by the ticking of the timer.

Allegra took a deep breath, struggling to ignore the pain of her strained shoulders. Quietly she murmured, "I guess he told us."

Simon shook his head ruefully. "I hate to admit it, but he's a damn good tactician. Crazy as a loon, but smart enough to have this figured out down to the last angle."

With that admission the last of Allegra's hope evaporated. She had been telling herself that there had to be a way out, something the Texan had overlooked. But if Simon didn't think so . . .

Gathering her courage, she whispered, "What do we do now?"

He looked surprised, as though the answer should have been obvious. "Get loose, of course. I don't know about you, but I can't defuse that bomb trussed up like a side of beef."

As she watched in mingled astonishment and disbelief, he began to swing in an increasingly wide arc until he came close enough to throw his ankles over the pipe and hoist himself up. From there it appeared a relatively simple matter for him to make his way down its length until he reached the joint where it connected with a larger conduit.

"Any idea what's in this thing?" he asked.

"Cold water . . . I think."

"Not too bad, considering the alternatives. Wrap both hands around the pipe and hold on."

Allegra lost no time obeying. An instant later she was severely jarred as Simon threw his weight against the joint. It creaked, but did not give. After several more equally fruitless attempts, he asked, "How much do you weigh?"

"A–about one hundred and twenty-five, I guess. Why?"

"Oh, yeah? You don't look it."

"Is this really the time for a discussion of my figure?"

"No . . . can you work your way down to me?"

"I guess . . ." In the snug-fitting skirt there was no possibility of getting her ankles over the pipe as Simon had. The best she could do was to inch along as her arms and back shrieked in protest.

By the time she finally reached him, her breathing was labored and her wrists were chafed raw. Yet she managed to meet his worried look with a brave smile. "Let's get on with it."

He hesitated a moment, then abruptly nodded. "Okay, on the count of three we pull down on the joint together. One . . . two . . . three . . ."

A crack appeared in the joint, emitting a small but steady stream of water. Twice more they bore down on the pipe, each time rewarded by a slight widening of the crack. Water was beginning to pool on the floor at their feet. The hem of Allegra's dress was wet, and Simon's pant cuffs were soaked through. "Again," he said.

The joint gave with a sharp, wrenching sound. A torrent of water gushed from the severed pipe, quickly drenching them. Cooled by the *Silver Zephyr*'s high altitude, the water was just slightly above freezing. It hit with an icy bite that numbed everything it touched.

But the packet of explosives left lying on top of a work table remained above the deluge, with its timer still inexorably ticking.

"Get out of here!" Simon yelled as he headed toward it. "There are only four minutes left."

"I'm not leaving. We're both still cuffed. You won't be able to manage alone."

"Allegra, do as I say!"

"We're wasting time. Forget me and concentrate on the bomb."

Recognizing the futility of arguing with her, Simon reluctantly did as she said. What he saw as he examined the weapon made him admit, if only to himself, that she had been right to stay.

"It's similar to the ones we put together in 'Nam. Two wires control the whole thing."

"Then you know how to defuse it?"

"Yes. There's just one problem. Depending on the exact structure of the bomb, the detonation wires have to be removed either in correct sequence or simultaneously. The wrong choice will cause it to blow at once."

Allegra swallowed hard. "Any idea which way this one is put together?"

"It's just a guess . . . but Fletcher mentioned the division he was with. They always wired for simultaneous detonation."

She met his eyes steadily. "Okay. I'll pull one and you pull the other."

The words came out a little muffled because her mouth had gone painfully dry, but their meaning was clear enough. Simon stared at her for a long moment, as though gauging the extent of her courage. Then he nodded.

"All right. Take hold of the one with the red tip." As she obeyed, his fingers closed around the adjacent wire. Together they braced themselves against the table.

One minute remained on the timer when he said, "Again on three. One . . . two . . . three . . ."

They pulled. Both wires came loose together. Allegra let out a low whistle of relief as Simon grinned broadly. But their relief was short-lived, lasting only until they realized that the detonator was still ticking.

Simon cursed low and eloquently. *"That s.o.b. . . . He booby-trapped it."*

"W-what . . . I don't understand . . ."

"Fletcher must have figured there was some chance I'd get loose, so he rigged it to make me think I knew how it was wired and cause me to waste time chasing down a blind alley." As he spoke Simon was hurriedly examining the bomb. Gingerly he pried off a small metal plate and peered into the cavity revealed beneath it.

"It's single wired . . . in there. Damn, my fingers won't fit!" Sweat was trickling down his forehead as he tried again to reach the wire. With his hands cuffed together he had little room to maneuver. Just as he had said, he couldn't reach inside the tiny opening.

Allegra glanced at the timer. Thirty seconds. The ticking seemed to be getting louder, filling the small room and reverberating off the metal bulkheads that would shortly be transformed into thousands of razor-sharp projectiles hurtling through space with the force of missiles.

She swallowed hard against the bile rising in her throat. Her hands, icy cold from the combination of freezing water and deadly terror, brushed his aside. "Let me. My fingers are smaller."

Reaching into the cavity, she made contact with the wire. Her first attempt to pull it free failed when her numb fingers slipped loose. She took a deep breath, willing herself to calmness. Ten seconds remained.

On the next try she managed to keep her hold on the wire, but it proved more difficult to detach than she had expected. "It's stuck to something," she gasped. "I can't get it loose."

"Pull hard!" Simon ordered. "There's no time."

Five seconds . . . four . . . three . . . two . . .

The wire popped free just as the last second ticked away. Allegra stared from it to the bomb and back again. A quivering weakness seemed to seize her as she swayed dazedly.

Simon was instantly at her side, propping her up with his body. "Easy, sweetheart. It's all over. You were great!"

His heartfelt praise and the heady grin he gave her convinced Allegra more eloquently than anything else that the danger really had passed. A long sigh escaped her as she let the wire drop. "That's cutting it about as close as I'd ever care to."

"Amen to that. But talk about coolness under fire . . . Are you sure you were never a marine?"

She laughed shakily. "Right now I'm not sure of anything except that I need to sit down."

"Go right ahead. I ought to be back soon."

"Back?"

"Fletcher," he reminded her gently. "I'd just as soon he didn't get away."

"Oh, Lord! I forgot about him! Come on, let's go."

"Honey, there's no reason for you to do anything more. Just stay here and rest. . . ."

"Simon York, will you please stop telling me what to do! You waste more time than any man I've ever known."

"Really?" he muttered under his breath as together they raced for the door. "And here I was thinking I was a pretty fast worker."

Allegra ignored him. There would be plenty of time later to hash out their relationship. All the problems and pitfalls she had imagined seemed singularly unimportant after their close brush with death. If they could overcome that together, then surely they could overcome anything.

But first they had to find Fletcher.

Reaching the main deck of the ship, they spotted Winston hurrying toward them with Kirsten at his side. "We've been looking everywhere for you," the Captain chided before he had quite taken in their bedraggled appearance. They had the satisfaction of seeing his mouth drop open as he registered the water-logged clothes, handcuffs and air of urgency. "What on earth . . . ?"

"Never mind about that," Simon said quickly. "The saboteur is Charlie Fletcher. He's probably already escaped, but we can at least try to find him. He planned to slide down one of the mooring ropes."

With the decisiveness ingrained by military training, Winston nodded instantly. "Of course. Kirsten, contact security and tell them what's happened. Call off the search for Mr. York and have all personnel concentrate on looking for Fletcher. Also alert the authorities on the ground."

Passengers on their way to dinner looked at them curiously. Allegra managed a bright smile that only bewildered them all the more. Murmuring to themselves, they disappeared around a corner.

"Contact that locksmith and have him meet us in the hold with metal cutters," Winston went on. Glancing at the handcuffs, he added, "Don't worry, we'll have those off in no time. But meanwhile, I suggest we track Mr. Fletcher."

"He may have gotten away by now," Allegra suggested worriedly as they hurried back to the hold. "Certainly he planned to."

"But he may have found his plans didn't work out too well," Simon told her reassuringly. "Getting to one of the mooring ropes couldn't be easy."

"Indeed not," Winston agreed. "We took extraordinary security procedures to safeguard them only an hour ago. By the way, do you happen to know anything about a burst water pipe?"

Briefly they told him what had happened along the catwalk. By the time they had finished they were at the starboard center of the vessel, near one group of mooring lines. There was no sign of Fletcher.

"We can't go racing all over the ship hoping to find him," Winston said. "Let's stop for a moment and try to figure out if he would have reason to select one particular line over the others.''

''He wouldn't want to be seen leaving,'' Simon pointed out, ''so he'd aim for the greatest camouflage.''

''On the way down that wouldn't matter. Even with the floodlights, he'd have plenty of shadow. But once he hit the ground . . .''

''He'd be looking for some kind of cover. . . .'' Allegra broke in. She closed her eyes for an instant, visualizing the field surrounding the *Silver Zephyr*. ''The bow! It's right over a copse of trees.''

It was a fact of which Charlie Fletcher was apparently well aware. They found him struggling with the metal plate securing the crawl space where the mooring ropes were fastened. His face was streaked with sweat and his eyes were wide with terror.

Allegra was surprised by his extreme distress, since he hadn't spotted them yet. It took a moment for her to realize the cause: The Texan was still on board after the time when the bomb was set to go off. He must have encountered far greater difficulty than he'd expected in getting at the mooring ropes, perhaps due to the extraordinary safeguards Winston had mentioned.

As the seconds ticked away, he would have known fear as great as their own. But whereas in their case the bomb's failure to detonate was an immense relief, for him it meant that capture would be imminent.

A look of exaltation flickered across his taut features as the plate at last gave way, exposing a portion of the ship's undercarriage. The wind blowing inward ruffled his hair and cooled his flushed features. He started to move forward, to let himself down along the rope that reached to freedom.

"Hold it, Fletcher!" Simon called. He moved forward to stop him, determined despite his cuffed hands.

Instead of obeying the Texan redoubled his efforts. He seemed oblivious to the futility of his actions. If he understood that he had run out of time, he didn't admit it even to himself.

The lower part of his body disappeared into the undercarriage. He grasped the rope tightly and flexed his broad shoulders inward so that they would fit through the small space.

"You can't make it!" Simon yelled. He was only yards away and closing fast, but Fletcher still seemed determined to ignore him. His torso began to disappear.

Allegra watched in unwilling fascination. To her exhausted senses both the Texan and Simon appeared to be moving in slow motion. Every detail was finely etched in her mind. She saw the grim anger evident in Simon's powerful body, the panic seeping into Fletcher's eyes, the moment when the outcome hung in the balance as the last remnants of his reason battled for control of his will. Battled and lost . . .

He moved jerkily, without thought for the slipperiness of the ropes. They were made to be controlled by electric winches, not pulled on by frantic hands damp with sweat. He misgauged his hold by a fraction, just enough for the ropes to suddenly pull loose. . . .

Simon lunged. He was close enough to catch him, but the handcuffs stopped him. His fingers brushed against Fletcher's face, frozen in an endless scream. Then the Texan was gone, falling away down the rope chute, ejected from the *Silver Zephyr* like a tiny organism repelled by a body it had tried to harm.

The scream heightened in pitch, drawing out to a keening wail as the distance increased, until at last there was only the rushing of the wind and the soft, barely audible murmuring of the great ship.

Chapter 14

"You must not blame yourself, Monsieur York," the French police inspector said. "You did everything possible to save him."

Simon nodded, though his expression remained bleak. Fletcher's body had been recovered from the copse of trees and taken away to a morgue. The authorities had come and gone, all except for the inspector, who lingered a few moments to shake his head in amazement over the tragedy that had been so nearly avoided.

"Only a madman could seek to destroy so glorious a vessel," he said. "It would have been a terrible disaster, not only because of the loss of life, but because of the waste of such beauty."

No one had the energy to point out to him that the *Silver Zephyr* might yet suffer for the attempted sabotage. There had been no possibility of keeping the events of that evening secret, nor would any of them have tried to do so. The passengers, and the public at large, had a right to know what had almost occurred. It remained to be seen how they would react.

So far at least there was one good sign: The passengers had taken the whole thing with remarkable calm due to the swift measures Winston had put into effect to assure them that it was understood who was responsible.

With Allegra's help he had drafted a brief statement which was then run off in the small printing shop on board and posted prominently throughout the vessel. It notified the passengers that departure from Cannes would be delayed until the following day, and why.

By the time it was read there was a general awareness on board that something very serious had happened. The disclosure that one of the backers had been responsible had an unexpectedly reassuring effect. Apparently most people thought that was better than a simple accident, or an act of terrorism, because it was far less likely to ever be repeated.

Confidence in the *Silver Zephyr*'s safety was, if anything, higher than ever. Which was ironic, considering how worried they had all been. Levinson and Rutherford still looked decidedly gray, and not only because they had come so close to losing their lives. Allegra was certain they weren't able to cope with that reality yet. They were too busy thinking about what else had almost gone up in flames, namely several million of their dollars.

In the aftermath of the near-tragedy they were happy

enough to accept Winston's authority without further challenge. Which was just as well, since he was very much in charge.

With Kirsten at his side he had met the authorities before touring the vessel to make sure there was no damage and everything was running smoothly. They made a good team, Allegra mused as she glanced at the tall, silver-haired captain and vivacious purser. Their manner made it clear each respected the other's abilities. On a more personal note, her perceptive eye picked out the discreet signs of genuine affection that presaged well for their future relationship.

If only her dealings with Simon were as simple. Having discovered that she loved him, she was more anxious than ever for some sign from him that their lives on opposite sides of the continent would not keep them irrevocably apart.

Common sense told her this was not the time to try to resolve so crucial an issue. But after the terror of the last few hours, rationality was all but beyond her. She was exhausted in mind and body, in desperate need of reassurance.

Instead she got comfort, which turned out to be almost as good. Simon was still talking with the inspector when he unexpectedly glanced up, meeting her eyes. For a moment he merely stared at her blankly until details of her appearance penetrated the fog of his own weariness and spurred him to action.

"If you don't mind," he told the police officer, "I'd prefer to answer any further questions you have at another time. Miss Whitney and I need to get out of these wet clothes."

The Frenchman eyed them both tolerantly. "Forgive me, I wasn't thinking. I will have statements drawn up for you both to sign tomorrow, but in the meantime there is nothing more to keep you here."

That was all Simon needed to know. He took Allegra's hand in his, ignoring her protests that she was really all right. "Kirsten, would you send some soup, sandwiches and brandy down to Miss Whitney's stateroom?" His face tightened as he noted the abrasions on her wrists. "Also bandages and antiseptic cream."

"The doctor would be happy to drop by," Winston pointed out.

"Thanks, but we can manage." He guided Allegra toward the stairs as she muttered, "I'm not some child with a scraped knee, you know. If I need looking after, I'll say so. And I'm not hungry; that food will go to waste."

"Maybe, but you should try to eat before you fall asleep."

"I'm not the least bit tired."

Ignoring her petulance, he nodded soothingly. "Of course you aren't. You get threatened by guns, hung from pipes and nearly blown to smithereens all the time. There's no reason for that to wear you out."

"Don't be sarcastic. I just resent being bossed around. I'm very independent . . . and used to taking care of myself . . . and . . ." She broke off, aware that she was beginning to shake and that her throat was tight with unshed tears.

"I know, Allegra," he murmured tenderly, opening the door to her stateroom, "but just this once let me take care of you instead."

Just this once? Was that really what he meant? It sounded so final, somehow, and so unbearably sad.

The tears began to flow in earnest, blurring her vision and turning her eyes to luminescent pools. She knew she was being foolish, behaving like a child. But she couldn't seem to help it. Suddenly she couldn't seem to do anything, even put one foot in front of the other.

But then she didn't have to, for Simon had seen her distress and was scooping her up in his powerful arms and carrying her into the bathroom, where he set her down gently and turned the hot water on in the shower. As the room quickly filled with steam, he began to matter-of-factly unfasten her dress.

"Don't . . . I can . . ."

"Hush, Allegra. You can barely stand."

That was true, but it didn't make it any easier to accept his impersonal care. He touched her as though she were an ailing child. There was no passion in the brush of his hands moving over her, slipping her dress down and discarding the lacy scrap of a bra she wore.

Lifting her free of the tangled clothes, he removed her last garment before she could gather her wits to object. Her nakedness added to the turbulence of her emotions made her unbearably vulnerable. Instinctively her hands moved to cover herself as she shook her head in mute rejection of being so exposed before him.

Simon groaned deep in his throat. "You're still fighting me, after all you've been through." With an impatient gesture he began to unbutton his shirt.

He didn't understand. It wasn't him she was fighting

but herself. The knowledge of how much he meant to her was not simply the illusionary by-product of being caught in a terrifying situation. Far from disappearing with the return of safety, it seemed to be growing with each passing moment, as though only that first tiny spark of awareness had been needed to turn it into a raging inferno.

Alone with him as she was, the fire threatened to singe her. How much worse it would be when he left and she fell headlong into the flames.

Fire and water . . . both hot. As Simon discarded the rest of his clothes and stepped into the shower with her, she turned her face away, letting the fine mist spray over her numbed skin. She wanted to be warm, needed it desperately, yet she didn't want to feel again, not any more than she could help.

Nothing was working out the way she wanted. Silly to say that when they were all still alive and the *Silver Zephyr* intact. She should be grateful, not frightened and uncertain. But she couldn't muster the right emotions.

A new, contrary self seemed to have taken up residence inside her. The woman who loved Simon was all she had ever been and more. It was the added part, the capacity to commit herself deeply and truly, that made her responses those of a stranger.

She would have to adjust, find some way to live with her new self and with whatever happened between her and Simon. And she would, as soon as she had a little more strength.

His hands were on her shoulders, turning her gently.

She didn't want to look at him, but that didn't seem to matter. He filled her eyes just as he had only hours before filled her body.

What right did he have to be so devastatingly attractive? Hadn't the man ever heard of restraint? He had a desk job, for heaven's sake. He should be flabby and out of shape, not endowed with an athlete's sculpted shoulders and arms, a virile chest covered by glistening chestnut hair, a flat abdomen, and long, strong legs corded with muscle.

He looked like something straight out of her fantasies, but he was breathtakingly real and compellingly male. Helplessly she swayed toward him, needing to feel the comforting strength of his body. He wrapped his arms around her as naturally as though he had done so every day of his life.

Cradling her gently, he murmured, "Feeling better?"

That wasn't exactly how she would describe it. She was still infinitely confused and frightened of what might lie ahead. Yet within his embrace she could not believe that anything would ever hurt her. The sensation of utter safety was highly seductive. Sighing softly, she gave herself up to it.

"You're almost out on your feet," he teased a moment later. "Bed for you."

Lifted from the shower, she was toweled dry with swift tenderness. As he bent to wipe the droplets of moisture from her slender legs, she stared down at him bemusedly and said the first thing that came into her head. "Children."

He glanced up, meeting her eyes. "What's that?"

"You'd be good with children. You're very . . . capable. . . ."

Simon straightened and reached for the robe hanging on the back of the door. He smiled slightly as he wrapped it around her. "Thanks, but I think it's only fair to tell you that I don't think of you as a child."

Allegra blinked sleepily. "How do you . . . think of me . . . ?"

He didn't answer at once but instead picked her up and carried her back to the bedroom. Setting her down carefully on the plush carpet, he kept an arm around her as he pulled the bedspread out of the way.

Having removed the robe, he eased her between the covers. The sheets were cold. She stiffened and instinctively hugged herself under the blanket. Simon switched off the light and began to move away. She was sure he meant to get dressed and leave.

"Don't go." The words were out before she could stop them. She closed her eyes in dismay. When she opened them again Simon was standing beside the bed with a towel wrapped around his lean waist and a concerned look on his face.

"I'm not going anywhere. Just lie back and take it easy. Everything will be all right."

Strange that he had phrased it that way; not everything *is* all right, but will be. As though he understood that the crisis they had passed through earlier was only the beginning of the trouble they faced.

A knock at the door prompted her to snuggle farther down under the covers. Simon went to answer it, returning with a tray laden with soup, sandwiches, brandy and first-aid supplies.

Sitting down beside her, he gently coaxed her arms out of hiding. "Let me see your wrists."

"They're fine."

"Humor me."

Reluctantly she did so, surprised by the red welts darkening her fair skin. They must hurt like the dickens, yet she hadn't even been aware of them.

Simon winced when he saw the damage done by the handcuffs. Carefully he dabbed on the soothing cream, then wrapped each wrist in gauze. Finished, he reached for the brandy and poured several inches of amber liquid into each of two crystal goblets.

"Here. You have to eat, too, but a little of this won't hurt."

Allegra smiled wanly. "If I drink all that you may have to feed me."

"I'll risk it." His gaze was very tender as he placed the glass in her hand and raised it to her lips.

She sniffed appreciatively, then took a tentative sip. It slid down her throat like liquid fire, warming her all the way through. Taking another, she accepted the sandwich he held out.

The paper thin slices of ham were faintly sweet, seasoned with honeyed mustard and pressed between halves of a fresh-baked croissant. For someone who had claimed only a short time before to have no appetite, she managed to make short work of it and another.

Simon grinned as he offered her a cup of fragrant clam chowder. Licking a crumb from the corner of her mouth, Allegra shook her head. "No, thanks. I'm filling up fast."

"Finish the brandy, then."

She glanced at the snifter dubiously, then shrugged and emptied it in a single long drink. A terrible waste of good brandy, but well worth the sacrifice. A pleasant woolliness descended on her, making her yawn deeply.

Simon took the empty glass from her, setting it along with his on the bedside table. He switched off the lamp and turned back to her. Again Allegra thought he meant to leave. Again a panicky need to stop him made her speak, but this time the words were only a muted sigh.

Her eyelids flickered as she fought the irresistible pull of sleep. She was losing the battle, drifting away in a cocoon of unconsciousness, when she felt the covers rise and a whisper of cool air touch her skin.

It was enough to revive her momentarily. Simon had tossed off the towel and was slipping into the bed beside her. He slid an arm beneath her, lifting her slightly so that he could draw her close.

Her head nestled on his chest as his big hands splayed gently over her back. His breath ruffled her hair as he murmured, "Go to sleep now."

The last of her resistance crumbled as though it had never been. The sweet languor of dreams stole over her, muting the fearful memories of the day and offering a gentle balm to her frayed emotions. She smiled against his skin as she yielded to oblivion.

Far into the night Allegra came awake with a suddenness that surprised her. She lay on her side, blinking at the darkness and wondering what had disturbed her rest.

The answer was readily apparent. So long as she was exhausted, she could lie next to Simon contentedly. But as soon as sleep had revitalized her body and healed her spirit, she was vividly, achingly aware of him. The deadening fatigue of a few hours before was gone, replaced by a renewed sense of energy and determination that reassured her that she was not becoming lost to herself after all.

They were pressed together spoon-fashion, the thick mat of hair on his chest tickling her back, and the hardness of his thighs curved round her buttocks. One sinewy arm lay over her waist, the hand lightly brushing her breasts.

Allegra glanced down, watching the rapid tautening of her nipples as the full impact of his presence reached her. She inhaled sharply. Hardly aware that she did so, she moved her hips against him provocatively.

Simon murmured in his sleep. His arm tightened around her, drawing her closer. She turned her head slightly, enough to see his relaxed features. Thick chestnut lashes lay on his burnished cheeks. The hard lines of his mouth were softened, making him look much younger and unexpectedly vulnerable. She wanted to touch that mouth with her own, to wake him gently and find again the blissful exaltation only he could give.

But she told herself that he needed his rest. After all, he had been through a grueling experience, made all the worse by the suspicion so unjustly leveled against him. Remembering that caused her to frown.

In those few minutes when they had stood together on the catwalk, before Fletcher had found them, he had said something about her not trusting him. As she recalled she had made a mess of correcting him. Did he still truly believe she had blamed him for the sabotage?

Allegra mulled that over for a few minutes before rejecting the possibility. If he thought that, he wouldn't have taken care of her so tenderly or stayed with her throughout the night. No, somewhere in the course of defusing the bomb and tracking Fletcher, he must have realized he had her complete trust . . . and more.

That being the case, what harm could there be in reconfirming what he already knew?

Squinting slightly, she focused on the little portable travel clock propped up on the bedside table. The luminescent dial read 5:15. That decided her. It wasn't as though it was still the middle of the night.

Without disturbing his arm, she managed to turn over so that she was facing him. Wiggling a few inches closer, she stopped only when they were touching all along the length of their bodies. Very softly she murmured, "Simon . . ."

Nothing. Maybe she was being a little too coy. Raising a hand, she let it trail along his muscular shoulder as she whispered, "Are you planning to sleep all day?"

"H'rumph . . . what'zit?"

So articulate. No wonder she loved him. Grinning, she leaned forward and with her tongue sought out the sensitive lobe of his ear. "Time's awastin', Simon. Up and at 'em."

His nose wrinkled. He mumbled something deep in

his throat and turned over on his back, drawing her with him. Propping herself up on his chest, she gazed at him vexedly. The man could sleep through an earthquake. Just what did it take to wake him?

A mischievous gleam lit her hazel eyes as she considered the obvious solution. For a moment she hesitated, torn between her desire to please both herself and him, and her instinctive shyness. Desire won.

Slipping sinuously down his length, she ducked under the covers, into a dark, warm nest musky with the scents of their bodies. Working her way down to the foot of the bed, she lightly kneaded the soles of his feet before dropping teasing kisses upward along his powerful calves and thighs.

In the darkness she had to rely on her sense of touch to experience his body. Her impression that he was in superb condition was certainly correct. Everywhere she touched she found tensile steel lightly covered by warm, smooth velvet.

Soft, curling hairs brushed against her cheek as she tentatively slipped her hands under his legs and let her fingers explore the skin of his inner thighs. With exquisite sensuality made possible by her love, she learned him in ways he already knew her, finding the unbridled male power of him a heady spur to her own arousal.

Through all this Simon didn't move or make a sound. Were it not for the hardening of his body she might have thought him completely unaware. Yet that he most certainly was not. Was it possible he was still asleep?

Driven by her curiosity, she poked her head out

from under the blankets, only to find him eying her with a blatantly male smile of approval. Innocently he said, "Oh, it's you."

Allegra very deliberately tightened her hand, causing him to wince in mock dismay. "Sorry about that," he said hastily. "Just a little joke."

"Very little." Her effort at sternness fled as she returned his smile. "Unlike something else I could mention."

"You did say up and at 'em," he reminded her with a touch of pardonable smugness.

"You were awake. Faker!" Playfully she scratched the nails of her other hand along his chest.

"Who, me? I just wanted to give you free rein. But now that I see where that leads . . ." Cupping the back of her head, he turned suddenly, reversing their positions. As he loomed above her, big and hard and male, and infinitely precious to her, he murmured, "You turn into a seductress, ready and willing to drive a man wild."

Allegra moved under him languidly. "Is that what I am?"

His smile faded, replaced by a look of such unbridled passion that she swallowed hastily. "Oh, yes," he said huskily, "that's what you are. A wild, beautiful seductress. And I can't get my fill of you."

His legs tangled with hers as he pressed her farther into the mattress, his hands circling lightly around her breasts. "Each taste of you only increases my hunger, until now I'm ravenous."

His words, his touch, the bold male strength of him hard against her, all combined to set off a tremor deep within Allegra. It rushed outward in rippling circles, as though a stone had cleaved the water of a tranquil pond.

She felt anything but tranquil as his mouth found hers, his lips urging hers apart for the questing entry of his tongue. Before when they had made love Simon had gone slowly, raising her from pinnacle to pinnacle of passion with steady expertise. But this time he was clearly as overcome by need as she was herself, so much so that he could not hold back very long.

Through the overwhelming force of her own passion Allegra felt the desperation in him and was moved by it. He thought she wasn't ready, but he was wrong.

Delicately she shifted against him to let him know there was no need to delay. Her arms wrapped around his neck as she brought her mouth back to his, stroking his tongue with her own. A spasm of pure longing raced through him. Responding to it, she brushed her breasts repeatedly back and forth across his chest, and deliberately raised her lower body to meet the thrusting force of his manhood.

Passion-glazed eyes stared down at her as he muttered, "Allegra . . . ?"

"Please, Simon," she groaned. "Don't wait any longer. I can't bear it."

That was all he needed to know. With a low growl he brought them together, filling her to such stunning completeness that the world narrowed down to only the two of them and the magic they were creating.

Once snugly lodged within her body, he recaptured his self-control. Slow, driving thrusts brought her to a fever pitch. She threw her head back, her hands clasping him urgently. *"Simon!"*

"Let me, angel," he rasped. "I want you to have everything . . . feel everything. . . ."

She couldn't bear any more. The shimmering pleasure that engulfed her was already so intense that she felt taken out of herself, hurtled into a realm of pure sensation where every nerve ending was exquisitely alive and screaming for satisfaction.

Desperately she tried to tell him, but words were beyond her. She could communicate only with her body, grasping him tightly within her in convulsive spasms as the world exploded and she was pierced by endless shards of ecstasy.

Barely had she begun to recover when she felt Simon tumble over the edge, his hoarse groan of pleasure bringing a new level of meaning to her own fulfillment.

Dazed but joyful, she joined him in the slow spiral back to earth, where the billowing glow of utter contentment awaited them. Entwined in a tender embrace, they drifted into the dreamless sleep of satiated lovers.

Allegra's last thought was that when morning really did come, they would talk. His tender care and enthralling lovemaking had given her the courage to openly admit her feelings and ask for the commitment she now was reasonably sure he would willingly give. When she woke, they would settle everything.

But she was wrong, for by then he was gone.

Chapter 15

"YOU SHOULDN'T BE IN ANY RUSH TO GET BACK TO work, Tristan," Allegra said. "Everything is coming along quite smoothly."

The tall, lean man in the chair across from her ran a hand through his umber hair and sighed. "This will sound terrible, but I almost wish there were problems just so I'd have an excuse to get back into action."

"It won't hurt you to rest for a few more days," she pointed out gently. "You've been through a rough time."

In fact, she was surprised to find Tristan looking as good as he did. The concussion he'd suffered in the car accident and the complications that followed when he insisted on checking out of the hospital prematurely would have kept most other men flat on their backs for weeks. But he was already at the point where he could spend a few hours each day working in the home office of his sprawling contemporary overlooking Long Island Sound.

Not having known precisely what she would encounter when she arrived at the house, Allegra had been very relieved to find him so well off. Despite all he had been through, he continued to look out at the world through startlingly light green eyes that held a decidedly mischievous gleam. His nose was long and straight, his mouth narrow, but still capable of frequent smiles. A solidly square chin hinted at the stubbornness with which he tackled his many and varied projects, all the results of his remarkable intellect.

To people meeting him for the first time he came as a great surprise. Instead of the solemn, self-absorbed technocrat they expected, they found themselves confronted by a man who might best be described as a very tall leprechaun.

Even in the face of his current boredom, an air of magical whimsy still hung about him. Sitting across from him in one of the comfortable leather chairs that dotted his study, Allegra could almost feel his powerful, restless mind searching for distraction.

"Even when I do get back to the office," Tristan mused, "I'm not sure how involved I'll be with the *Silver Zephyr*. You have everything so well in hand that I might as well move on to a fresh idea."

"I am a little surprised by the response to what happened in Cannes," Allegra admitted. "Not only did the passengers who were on board at the time decide the ship was safe, but that seems to be the view taken by the public at large. Since the story broke we've been snowed under by requests for tickets to the point where we're now booked solidly through the next six months.''

''Not exactly what Fletcher had in mind.''

''I should say not. Tristan . . . something occurred to me a couple of days ago. Has anyone suggested to you that he might have been behind your accident? After all, having you laid up back here and unable to make the trip could have worked to his benefit.''

''Funny you should ask that. I had a chat with a couple of detectives earlier in the week. They're taking a new look at my car to determine if anyone fooled with it. From what I've heard so far, it looks as though the brakes may have been jimmied.''

Allegra shook her head in dismay at how far the Texan had been willing to go to save himself. ''Of course, he couldn't have expected you to send someone in your place.'' She broke off, inwardly berating herself for stumbling onto that line of thought.

Ever since waking that morning ten days before in Cannes to find Simon gone, she had resolutely tried to keep her mind on other things. The hurt was too great, the loss too profound to dwell on. Eventually she might be able to confront them, but not for quite a while.

Tristan watched her as she sat lost in thought, and his face softened. There was a great deal he understood without having to be told. Ever since Cannes, he had heard the tension in Allegra's voice and guessed that something far beyond the near-sabotage was bothering her. Now that she sat before him, looking unexpectedly fragile and vulnerable, he was able to make an educated guess about the source of the trouble.

Quietly he said, "Fletcher wasn't a man who would know very much about friendship. He couldn't have guessed that I had Simon to turn to."

"Yes, well, if that's all, I should really be going. . . ."

"Why in such a rush? Since everything's moving along smoothly, you don't have to dash back to the office any more than I do."

"Oh, but . . . there's a lot I need to take care of . . . detail stuff . . . you know . . ."

"Hmmm, I know an excuse when I hear it. Anybody would think you were anxious to battle the traffic back to the city." Though he said it humorously, the perceptive look in his eyes made Allegra uneasy. Tristan could get through her defenses almost as easily as Simon, though for completely different reasons.

Returning his look, she found herself wondering why the two of them had never passed beyond friendship. Tristan was an undeniably attractive man whose brilliance was matched by a genuinely caring, compassionate nature. Far from being egotistical about his intelligence, he was possessed of true affection for the rest of humanity. He was witty, urbane, charming and off-beat enough to be truly fascinating.

Somewhere there had to be a woman for whom he would be perfect. Given her present unhappiness, Allegra could only regret she wasn't it. Why had she had the great misfortune to fall in love with a man who could take her to the heights of passionate abandonment only to walk away without looking back?

To be fair, that wasn't completely accurate. Simon had left a note which she found on top of her bureau shortly after waking. The words were burned into her mind, yet she was no closer to making sense of them than she had been ten days before.

"I have to go back to California to take care of a business problem," he had written. "I'll be in touch soon."

Hardly the words of a lover. Or were they? After reading them over and over so many times, she might be putting too much into them, but it did seem to Allegra that such abruptness was unlike Simon. Angry and hurt though she was, she had to acknowledge that he was gentle and considerate, unlikely to wantonly hurt anyone, much less a woman with whom he had shared the heights of intimacy.

Why then had he left, and why had she still had no word from him? The questions tormented her, making the nights a long, empty struggle to court sleep that came only in the stingiest snatches, leaving her more exhausted and drained with each passing day.

If only there were someone she could ask . . . ? Glancing at Tristan speculatively, she caught him watching her with a tiny grin quirking his firm mouth. Sourly she muttered, "I don't see what there is to be amused about."

"No, I suppose you wouldn't. Very few of us have any idea how we appear to the rest of the world."

Allegra's eyebrows shot up challengingly. "What's that supposed to mean?"

"Only that ever since I first met you five years ago you have seemed to me to be the epitome of self-containment and assurance. You've always known what you wanted and gone after it in the most intelligent way possible. I admire you tremendously; that, in essence, is why I asked you to be part of the *Silver Zephyr* venture.''

His quiet praise, coming so unexpectedly, took Allegra aback. She was at a loss as to how to react. ''T–thank you . . . but I don't feel very assured these days, much less self-contained.''

Tristan's smile widened. ''I noticed that. Frankly, the change in you is fascinating. I've heard about it, of course, but this is the first time I've had the chance to observe it up close.''

''What's 'it'?''

He shrugged, as though the answer should be obvious to them both. ''Love, naturally.'' At her startled look he added, ''And it is natural, Allegra. A beautiful and very desirable part of being human. I rather envy you.''

''Envy? That's like saying you envy someone who's hanging off the edge of a cliff, or being swept away in a whirlpool, or . . .''

Tristan laughed gently. ''I get the picture. No one ever said the course was smooth.''

''And no one ever warned me it was strewn with land mines,'' she grumbled. ''I swear, if Simon were here right now, I'd . . .'' She blushed and looked away, embarrassed at having actually voiced his name.

''Simon is my friend,'' Tristan reminded her gently, ''but so are you. I hate for you both to be hurting like this.''

"What makes you think we both are? I have no reason to believe Simon loves me."

"Don't you?"

The quiet question brought her up short. Tristan had a point. Just because Simon hadn't said the words didn't mean he didn't feel the same way she did. The fact was that she hadn't told him, either.

But if he loved her, why had he gone, and why, especially, had she heard nothing from him?

"He's in California," she murmured, staring sightlessly out the window. "Something to do with a business problem, at least that's what he said."

Tristan nodded serenely. "He must have meant that microchip he was accused of stealing."

Allegra's eyes widened. She straightened in her chair and stared at him intently. "Microchip . . . ? Winston mentioned something to me about that. But surely he wouldn't go off and leave me because of that."

With some care Tristan rose from his chair and crossed the room to the oak cabinet set against one wall. Opening it, he revealed a small but fully stocked bar from which he selected a choice cognac. With a filled glass in each hand, he turned to Allegra and offered her one before settling himself back down.

"On the contrary, that's about the only reason I can think for him to be apart from you. You have to understand. Simon is an intensely proud man. It was pride that made him enlist in the marines and serve heroically in Vietnam despite his severe doubts about that war. Pride spurred him to start his own business and make a great success of it in a highly competitive field. He's built himself a good life, but there's no way he'd ask a woman to share it while there was any question of dishonor hanging over him.''

"But I could never believe he stole anything. I've known from the moment Winston mentioned it that Simon was innocent, just as I knew he had nothing to do with the sabotage.''

"You knew you felt that way, but did he?''

"Yes, of course . . . at least, I think he did. . . .''

"Wouldn't it be a good idea to be sure?''

The suggestion, offered so matter-of-factly, roared through Allegra's mind. She grabbed hold fiercely, wanting desperately to believe that so simple—and correctable—a reason lay behind Simon's absence. Even as the more logical side of her mind insisted it couldn't possibly be that easy, she had reached a decision.

"I do have to be sure . . . I can't stand this suspense. But there's only one way to end it. I have to see Simon.''

Tristan regarded her benignly, as though she were a prize student who had just lived up to all his expectations. After opening a drawer in the table beside him, he pulled out a small leather book and thumbed through the pages before handing it to her. "Here's his address.''

Allegra wasn't surprised that Simon lived not in the sterile environs of Silicon Valley, where the microchip industry was centered, but in San Francisco, easily one of her favorite cities.

She finished her drink, stood up and dropped a light kiss on Tristan's cheek. He promptly blushed, earning an indulgent chuckle from her. "Wait until this happens to you," she warned. "I'll sit back and enjoy every minute of it."

"Find me the right woman and you'll earn my eternal gratitude. But in the meantime, go get your own life straightened out."

With a smile and a wave she was gone, hurrying through the tiled foyer and down the gravel path to her car. For once the traffic back into the city was mercifully light. She made excellent time. Well before the onslaught of the rush hour she had reached her apartment, gotten a reservation on an evening flight to the coast and packed herself a bag.

The trip to the airport was slower and strained her nerves, but before she could bring herself to question too closely the wisdom of what she was doing, she was settled into a seat on a 747 headed west, enveloped in the welcome anonymity of strangers who could not have suspected that the quiet, composed young woman beside the window was embarked on a desperate gamble that would determine the future course of her life.

The flight arrived while it was still daylight. Allegra was blind to the beauty of San Francisco as her cab headed toward Simon's address. She had debated the merits of checking into a hotel instead, and calling him, but rejected that as cowardly.

If he was displeased to see her or—she cringed at the thought—if he was with someone else, she would just as soon have it all over and done with right then. Thinking about the possibilities of what she might confront made her stomach tighten painfully and set her head to throbbing. By the time the cab pulled up in front of a gracious row house on Nob Hill her palms were damp, and her knees showed a decided tendency to weakness.

She paid the driver and got out, then stood on the sidewalk looking up at the house. There was only one name on the bell beside the gracefully carved door: Simon's. Whatever problems he had encountered in his business, he had clearly also had enormous successes. His was not a neighborhood that attracted failures.

So how much trouble could he actually be in as long as there was no moving van parked in front and his name was still on the door? Figuring that it was time she found out, Allegra took a deep breath, gripped her suitcase in her hand and, by dint of putting one foot in front of the other, found herself within reach of the bell.

She pressed it gingerly. A soft peal sounded somewhere toward the back of the house. Holding her breath, she listened. Several moments passed before she heard the approach of firm footsteps.

"Yes, what is it . . . ?" Simon's voice trailed off. He stared at her in bewilderment, his brow knitting and his eyes dark with disbelief. "Allegra . . . ?"

Even dressed in worn jeans and a soft plaid shirt that had seen better days, he was breathtakingly attractive. She tried not to think about that as she said with forced lightness, "Hi, there. I happened to be in the neighborhood, so I thought I'd drop in."

At his quizzical look she shrugged. "No, that isn't it. I'm running away from home, and I thought you might want to adopt me." As he continued to stare she tried yet again. "I'm selling Girl Scout cookies. If you're nice to me, I'll throw in a box free."

Solemnly he said, "I don't think they're allowed to do that."

"What?"

"Girl Scouts. My niece is one. They aren't allowed to give deals." When she didn't answer he became aware that she was still standing on the doorstep and stood aside hastily.

"Come in. I'm . . . glad to see you."

That instant of hesitation was all the spur her insecurity needed. She stood in the foyer, still holding her suitcase as she stared unseeingly at the discreet collection of choice antiques. "You don't sound very sure."

"It's not that," he said, taking her bag. "I'm just surprised."

"I guess I should have called. . . ."

"No, that's okay. But it's a good thing you didn't get here a few hours from now, or we would have missed each other."

Not understanding, she followed the nod of his head and looked toward a suitcase standing at the foot of a curving marble staircase that led up to the second floor. "I'm booked on the red-eye flight to New York," he explained. "It looks as though you've saved me the trip."

"You were . . . going to see me . . . ?"

He frowned and took a step closer to her. "I said in the note I left that I'd be in touch soon." More urgently he added, "You did find my note, didn't you?"

"Oh, yes, on the bureau the next morning. I thought

it was a little . . . inadequate under the circumstances.''

Simon had the grace to look abashed. ''I knew that
at the time I wrote it, but I couldn't figure out what else
to do. If I'd woken you, you would have had questions
I couldn't answer, and leaving would have been all that
much harder.''

When she didn't comment, but waited for him to go
on, he gestured toward a graciously appointed living
room off the foyer. ''Let's sit down. Can I get you
anything? A drink, something to eat?''

Allegra shook her head. She couldn't have managed
either. Instead she took refuge in politeness. ''You
have a beautiful home.''

''Not what you expected, is it?'' Simon asked,
managing a tentative smile.

''To tell you the truth, I never thought much about it.
I guess there hasn't been time.''

''No, there hasn't, has there?'' He sat down beside
her on the wing-backed couch and gently took her hand
in his. Her skin was cold, her fingers stiff. Rubbing
them, he murmured, ''I like seeing you here, in my
home. It's very . . . reassuring. . . .''

She laughed nervously. ''It stands to reason I
wouldn't have come all this way if I'd decided I didn't
care about you.''

''But you do . . . care?''

''Yes, although I have to tell you I'm not too thrilled
about admitting it after the way you just left me
hanging out on a limb. Really, Simon, didn't you stop
to think how I'd feel?''

''Of course I did,'' he protested quietly. ''I haven't

thought about much else since I last saw you. That last night we spent together . . ." His eyes met hers tenderly, ". . . was the most beautiful of my life."

Allegra blinked quickly. His acknowledgment of what had passed between them meant a great deal to her. It gave her the courage to go on, even as it made her vividly aware of how unnecessary the last ten days had been. "Then why," she demanded almost angrily, "didn't you let me come back here with you? If Tristan's right, and you did come because of that silly microchip business . . ."

"You know about that?"

"Of course I do. Winston found out shortly after the first threats came in, and he warned me. He thought you might be a suspect."

"He did?"

"Well, I certainly didn't! Not from the beginning. How could you believe that I would have let you get so close to me if I had any idea you could be capable of doing something wrong?"

"I didn't believe that . . . exactly. But everything about you . . . about us . . . was so perfect that I was afraid to let myself accept it."

"So what were you planning to do, Simon? Drop in on me when you happened to be in New York?"

Now it was his turn to be offended. "That's not fair. How was I supposed to know you believed in me right from the start? I thought I still had some convincing to do."

"Well, you don't. I trust you completely, and I love you more than I ever thought it possible to love any—" She broke off, abruptly aware that Simon was staring at her with an expression that could only be called beatific.

He touched a long, tanned finger to her face with infinite gentleness. "You really love me?" The deep voice held an expression she had never heard before: wonder combined with happiness so profound that she knew it had to be the equal of her own.

Her breath left her in a long, shaky sigh. Tremulously she nodded.

Simon smiled whole-heartedly as his hand moved down to cup the nape of her neck and draw her to him tenderly. Against her mouth he shaped the words, "And I love you, Allegra Whitney, soon, I hope, to be Allegra York. You're all I've ever dreamed of and more. It's taken me a lifetime to find you, but now that I have, believe me when I say I will never let you go."

His kiss was long and deep, the familiar passion heightened and made all the more enthralling by their knowledge of the love they shared. She returned it unrestrainedly, withholding nothing from him as together they pledged themselves in a language that went beyond mere words into the realm of souls twining together for eternity.

When they at last drew some little way apart, Allegra leaned back in his arms and surveyed his features with the softly adoring gaze of a lover to whom everything is forever new, yet dearly familiar. It occurred to her that when she was a little girl she had sometimes wondered what the man she married would look like. Nothing in her imaginings had prepared her for the reality.

"Simon," she murmured as he again drew her to

him, "when we're settled wherever it is we're going to live, I'd like to invite Tristan to dinner."

"Of course," he agreed, busy nibbling at the delicate line of her throat. "After all, he is responsible for our getting together."

"Mmmm . . . I thought we'd invite my friend, Cassia Jones, too. They should meet."

He chuckled indulgently. "I guess it's true what people say. Once you fall in love you want the rest of the world to know the same joy."

"Exactly." He really was the most wonderful man, but he had a tendency sometimes to wear too many clothes. Like now. Her fingers went to work on the buttons of his shirt as she gazed up at him through the thick fringe of her lashes.

The pulse that leaped to life along his jaw fascinated her. Watching it, she barely heard him mutter, "I suppose we really should talk about the practicalities. I've sold my business here. I should be able to get rid of this house just as easily."

"Don't. I already love your home. Besides, I've been wanting to open a West Coast branch." Spreading the sides of his shirt apart, she bent her head to feather tiny kisses into the curling hairs of his chest. "My staff in New York can run that end of the business while I take care of more important things." Lest he be left in any doubt, she showed him exactly what she considered worthy of her attention.

Simon swallowed hard. "Don't you want to know how I settled that trouble over the chip?"

She glanced up for an instant. "If you want to tell me."

"I found the guy who had sold the chip to the company that was claiming ownership. Just as I'd suspected, he turned out to be a former employee of mine who had access to the early design phases of my work. When I confronted him with that yesterday he owned up and gave a statement completely exonerating me."

"Of course," Allegra murmured. "I knew it had to be something like that."

His hands brushed her shoulders through the silk of her blouse before drifting downward to gently cup her breasts. Beneath the sensual persuasion of his touch, her nipples grew taut and aching. Huskily he said, "You're very trusting."

"It goes along with being in love," she explained, shifting against him so that they were half-lying on the couch. Kicking off her shoes, she twined her legs with his.

Simon smiled down at her with such tenderness that her loving gaze shone with unshed tears. Seeing them, he kissed the corner of each eye, the straight line of her nose in between, and the curve of her chin. Brushing aside stray tendrils of rich brown hair, he caressed her brow before tracing the high arch of her cheekbones with his ardent mouth.

"When you're a very old lady," he murmured, "you'll still be beautiful."

Tracing the tensile cords of his back with soft, savoring caresses, she sighed contentedly. "And when you're a very old man I'll want you every bit as much as I do right now."

"That's good to hear," he teased while gently

pressing her further back into the couch. "By then we should have plenty of practice." His hands shook slightly as he pulled her blouse free of the waistband of her skirt. Allegra lay back, enjoying the slow buildup of anticipation as he undressed her.

When all but the lace scrap of her panties lay on the floor beside the couch, Simon moved away just long enough to remove the rest of his own clothes. The golden light of early evening, flowing in through the wide, tall windows, bathed the sculpted planes and angles of his magnificent body.

Her breath caught in her throat as she studied him. He was so overwhelmingly male, with all the strength and power of superb virility, yet he was also capable of infinite gentleness. He had the courage to defy wanton destruction and death, and to give his heart freely with a full measure of hope and pride.

The tormenting emptiness she had felt since being parted from him found its echo in the hungry yearning of his gaze as it swept over her. Seeing the look in his pewter eyes, she knew beyond doubt that he was as vulnerable in his own way as she was in hers. They could hurt each other badly, but instead they had chosen to cast aside personal defenses and take the ultimate risk of uniting two lives in a single future.

A future that glowed as brightly as the flame of passion raging between them. Her arms opened to welcome him back, the warm weight of his body sending tremors of delight through her. With sublime concentration she gave herself up to the shimmering spiral of desire.

Together they climbed higher and higher, bodies and

spirits cleaving in perfect harmony. Earthly barriers fell away as though they had never been. In a realm that only lovers reach, they sealed a pledge that would sustain them for all time.

Having dared to dream, they knew the ultimate joy of seeing the dream become reality. Having risked all, they were rewarded with the gift of joy beyond any they had ever imagined. Having stood firm against death, they celebrated the infinite beauty of life.

They had journeyed far from the worldly shallows of distrust and doubt, but for them love's greatest adventure had only just begun.

Silhouette Intimate Moments
Receive 2 Books Free!

Free-Books Certificate
MAIL TODAY To Reserve Your Home Subscription

Silhouette BOOK CLUB OF CANADA
320 Steelcase Rd. E., Markham, Ont. L3R 2M1

YES, please send me FREE, and without obligation, 2 exciting Silhouette paperback originals. Unless you hear from me after I receive my 2 FREE BOOKS, please send me 4 full-length, Silhouette Intimate Moments novels to preview each month, as soon as they are published. I understand that you will bill me just $2.50 each (a total of $10.00) with *no additional shipping, handling or other hidden charges.* There is no minimum number of books that I must buy, and I can cancel this arrangement anytime I wish. The first 2 books are mine to keep, even if I never take a single additional book.

Signature_____
(If under 18, parent or guardian must sign)

Name_____

Address_____

City_____

Prov. _____ Postal Code_____

2 FREE BOOKS NOW...
4 BOOKS DELIVERED RIGHT
TO YOUR HOME!

This offer limited to one per household, expires March 31, 1985. If price changes are necessary, you will be notified.

IM2F

Silhouette

Intimate 🌑 *Moments*

Have you missed any of these
bold . . . dramatic . . . passionate . . . and intense
Silhouette Intimate Moments novels?

Silhouette BOOK CLUB OF CANADA
320 Steelcase Road E., Markham, Ontario L3R 2M1

Please send me the books I have checked above. I am enclosing
a total of $_____ (Please add 75 cents for postage and
handling.) My cheque or money order is enclosed. (No cash or
C.O.D.'s please.)

Name_____

Address _____ Apt____

City _____

Province _____ Postal Code_____

Prices subject to change without notice. (DBIM1)

Silhouette Desire

Receive 2 Books Free!

Free-Books Certificate
MAIL TODAY To Reserve Your Home Subscription

Silhouette BOOK CLUB OF CANADA
320 Steelcase Rd. E., Markham, Ont. L3R 2M1

YES, please send me FREE, and without obligation, 2 exciting Silhouette paperback originals. Unless you hear from me after I receive my 2 FREE BOOKS, please send me 6 full-length, Silhouette Desire novels to preview each month, as soon as they are published. I understand that you will bill me just $2.25 each (a total of $13.50) with *no additional shipping, handling or other hidden charges.* There is no minimum number of books that I must buy, and I can cancel this arrangement anytime I wish. The first 2 books are mine to keep, even if I never take a single additional book.

Signature_____
(If under 18, parent or guardian must sign)

Name_____

Address _____

City_____

Prov. _____ Postal Code_____

2 FREE BOOKS NOW...
6 BOOKS DELIVERED RIGHT TO YOUR HOME!

This offer limited to one per household, expires March 31, 1985. If price changes are necessary, you will be notified.

D2FI